17 MONTHS AND A SECRET

MAXINE CABRALL

What the Readers Said

Reviews:

"Seventeen Months and a Secret" is more than just a suspense novel—it's a powerful story and a film in the making. I can only imagine the months of anxious reflection, the countless moments of doubt, and the internal questions—"*Am I really doing this?*"—leading up to that pivotal deep breath, followed by the exhale that birthed a ministry for so many.

Every chapter is a testament to courage, raw transparency, and deep emotion. To call this work excellent is an understatement—it will leave you breathless with the sheer mastery of its storytelling. I am beyond proud of you, Maxine.

Marlon R. Nicolls CEO, Nicolls Media Group

To me, this book didn't tell the story of a man grappling with homosexual urges; it told the story of a Christian man who deeply believes in God and is willing to fight to align his life with his faith. In a world where society often tells us that we are somehow "wired wrong" if our desires don't perfectly align with our beliefs, you've shown that the real journey is in acknowledging those struggles and choosing to face them head-on, with honesty and faith.

Your willingness to be open with your wife about something so challenging is incredibly inspiring. It's a reminder that the first step toward healing and growth in any relationship is honesty, no matter how difficult it may be. By trusting God and being forthright, you've set an example that many others can look up to.

Thank you for your bravery and for showing others that even in the face of such trials, God does not make mistakes. You are helping others see that it's possible to confront our deepest struggles while staying committed to our faith, our partners, and the life God has called us to live.

Your story is not just one of challenges but of hope, redemption, and unwavering faith. I believe it will inspire many to be honest with themselves and their loved ones and to trust in God's perfect plan.

Anonymous

I finished reading your book, and I wanted to let you know how deeply it moved me. Your honesty and vulnerability in sharing the challenges you faced in your marriage were both courageous and inspiring. I appreciated

how you didn't shy away from the difficult moments but instead provided a real and raw account of what you went through. It made the story so relatable and powerful.

I have to tell you, this is the first book I've finished in over five years, and I completed it in less than 24 hours. I was up late because I just couldn't put it down! Your writing drew me in from the very first page, and I found myself deeply invested in your journey.

Your ability to persevere and stay committed to your marriage, even when things were incredibly tough, is a testament to your strength and faith. I found myself reflecting on the importance of communication, patience, and understanding in relationships. Your journey is a beautiful reminder that while marriage isn't always easy, the hard work and dedication are worth it.

Thank you for sharing your story with the world. I know it will help so many others who might be going through similar struggles. It's a powerful reminder that with love, resilience, and faith, we can overcome the toughest of times.

Anonymous

As I reflect on this book, I have to say that, even though I'm not married, it deeply resonates with my own

struggles in past relationships—whether romantic or otherwise. The themes and lessons within it felt incredibly relatable to the challenges I've faced with various people in my life. What really struck me was how the book helped me gain a new perspective on how I interact with others and what I might be like from their point of view. From the very first page,

I was completely hooked, and I ended up finishing the entire book in a single afternoon. It left me wanting more, like a meal that satisfies but doesn't quite fill you up.

My only regret is the self-contained nature of the story. I wish there was more, perhaps a sequel, because if there were, I'd buy it without hesitation. This book has the kind of insight that deserves to be shared widely, and I truly believe it should be adapted into other formats so its powerful lessons can reach as many people as possible.

Anonymous

Although riveting, the writer takes an unflinching look at her relationship, marriage, and the seismic shift that occurs 17 months into the union. From the beginning, the narrative is imbued with emotional honesty.

The rawness, vulnerability, and transparency revealed as you turn each page would only increase your love and appreciation for the couple.

Thank you for sharing such intimate moments of your life. I pray that God will continue to bring healing and comfort and an immeasurable level of success today and every day. A must-read!

Kathy Hicks

Dedicated to: - Carl, I'm excited about what God has done, is doing and will do with and through us

Foreword by Dr Cheryll Holmes PhD PsyD

"Seventeen Months and a Secret" is more than just a story about Maxine and Carl, it reflects the experiences of many Christian couples who face silent struggles with their faith and personal challenges. This book takes us into the private battles that emerge when same-gender attraction complicates a marriage, highlighting the often- unseen pain of those who lack the support they need during their most vulnerable moments. It is not that their community did not want to help, but they did not know how to.

As I read through these pages, it became clear that Maxine and Carl each carry their own burdens. Initially, I felt a profound sympathy for Maxine, deeply moved by her confusion and heartbreak. But as the story unfolded, Carl's pain became equally apparent. He had kept a significant struggle hidden from Maxine—his personal battle with same-gender attraction. This was not an external foe but an internal conflict that he faced in isolation, grappling with desires that clashed with his faith, and sometimes succumbing to them.

Instead of finding understanding and grace, Carl faced judgment. Those around him, perhaps grappling with their own issues, saw his struggle as particularly severe. Yet, in reality, his struggle was akin to the challenges we all encounter—resisting temptation and sometimes falling short.

This narrative offers a profound lesson: we must learn to differentiate between those who are earnestly fighting their inner battles and those who have given in to their sins. Carl bore his secret alone for far too long, and as a community, we failed to support both him and Maxine adequately, not because of ill heartedness but out of ignorance, we didn't know how. As I read this book I actually "saw" the scale that sin is put into and there is an imbalance that we have ignored. For many of us as members of the clergy, homosexuality "weighs" more than any other sin, more than adultery, fornication, stealing, covetousness, etc. The book highlights that there is still so much work for us to do because there is no such 'scale' with God.

Despite these shortcomings, God's grace has helped this couple find their way through. Their story is one of resilience, grace, and redemption. It reminds us to offer compassion rather than judgment and to understand that no

struggle is beyond the reach of divine grace. This is a story that deserves to be shared, and I am honored to introduce it to you.

— Rev. Dr. Cheryll Holmes, PhD, PsyD

Table of Contents

CHAPTER 1:

My Friends Thought He Was the One

It was a serene Sunday morning, and our church was a buzz with the usual hum of congregants gathering for the weekly service. I had settled into my usual spot among a close-knit group of friends. The sermon had begun, and I found myself absorbed in the words being shared. It was one of those moments where I was completely lost in the message, feeling everything align perfectly.

Then, I felt it—a series of gentle nudges on either side of me. My friends, always a source of light-hearted mischief, were giving me playful elbow jabs. Their eyes twinkled with a mix of amusement and anticipation. I turned to them, puzzled by their sudden urgency. They were gesturing subtly toward the pulpit, and that's when I noticed him—a tall, attractive, somewhat reserved man moving through the crowd with quiet grace.

He was new to our community, having recently joined

from another ministry. His arrival had stirred some curiosity, and as he walked past, there was a noticeable buzz of whispers. He wasn't strikingly handsome in a conventional sense, nor did he have the charismatic flair that often draws immediate attention. Instead, he carried himself with an understated confidence that was both intriguing and slightly aloof.

My friends' grins widened, and one of them leaned in, whispering in a conspiratorial tone, *"That's your husband."*

I chuckled softly, shaking my head in disbelief. *"No way,"* I replied, though a spark of curiosity was lit. At that moment, he seemed more like a distant figure than a potential partner. His demeanor was quiet, almost reserved, and he avoided making direct eye contact. Some in our congregation had noted his reluctance to engage fully, interpreting it as aloofness, maybe even arrogance.

He seemed to be navigating a new environment—unfamiliar, perhaps even daunting. I sensed an air of solitude around him, a palpable loneliness. While I didn't feel an immediate connection or attraction, I felt drawn to the idea of offering a welcoming gesture. Yet a part of me hesitated. I wasn't one to pursue someone, or so I told myself.

Weeks passed, and our interactions remained polite but distant. He attended events and joined in discussions, but always with a certain detachment. My friends, undeterred, continued their playful jabs, hinting that there was more to our encounters. Their teasing became a mild source of frustration, making me wonder if there was some hidden truth beneath their banter.

Despite their encouragement, I wasn't actively seeking a relationship. My life was fulfilling in its own right, and I had been contentedly single for several years. I had even reached a point where I told God that if He intended for me to remain single, I would accept it with grace. This period of self-reflection and acceptance was important to me, and I'd made peace with it.

He attended college out of state and visited the church when he could. One weekend, during one of his visits, our leader asked us to bless him monetarily. After he returned to college, I sent him an encouraging note with $50 enclosed. He later told his roommate that there was something different about my letter. We often joked that I had paid $50 for him.

As time went on, I noticed him becoming more comfortable within our community. His initial shyness began to dissipate, though he still carried an air of mystery. I found myself increasingly curious about him. What was behind that quiet exterior? Was he interested in me, or simply seeking friendship? Or maybe he just needed a ride home?

One of the most puzzling aspects was his approach to communication. Our conversations, when they happened, were often brief and surface-level. He seemed more interested in maintaining a polite distance than building a connection. This made me question whether my frustration was rooted in unmet expectations—or perhaps a deeper desire for a meaningful relationship.

Rumors began to circulate within our community. It was said that he had inquired about me, stirring a mix of hope and frustration within me. I found myself grappling with growing feelings for him, even as his feelings remained elusive. His deep love for God, his intelligence, and his unique talents were qualities that fascinated me. Yet, despite these positive traits, any hint of his romantic interest remained frustratingly vague.

One Christmas, our community organized a secret gift exchange. I drew his name, and I was thrilled at the opportunity to give him a thoughtful gift. I chose a camera, knowing he had a budding interest in photography. I hoped this gesture would open the door for a deeper conversation. The gift exchange went well, and he expressed genuine appreciation for the camera. It was a small victory, but it didn't seem to lead to anything beyond polite gratitude. A few years later, I became his top model.

My friend, who had been a source of support and guidance throughout this process, was ecstatic for me. She had been married for years and often offered valuable advice on relationships. When he called to thank me for the gift, I felt a sense of warmth and connection. However, it was clear that the gift alone wasn't enough to bridge the gap between us. His calls were polite but didn't lead to further engagement.

Then came a winter evening that became a turning point. After dropping him off at home, I discovered he had left his hat in my car. It was a seemingly insignificant event, but I chose to see it as a sign. Placing his hat on my head, I jokingly declared, *"Just as he wore this hat, so shall the owner of this hat become the head of my household."* This playful declaration symbolized my faith and hope for our future.

Eventually, I reached a point where I could no longer tolerate the ambiguity. I needed clarity on where we stood. I was determined to have a direct conversation with him about our relationship. I wanted to know if he was interested in pursuing something more or if I should move on. The thought of this conversation filled me with both anticipation and anxiety. One Sunday, I went to his office to tell him I needed to speak with him. My heart skipped a few beats, and I was nervous, hoping he wouldn't see it. My knees were shaking, and sweat was about to break out. I entered the office as bold as a lion, but he immediately stopped me, saying, *"I need to speak with you."* He knew precisely why I was there; the look on my face said it all.

When we finally spoke, he shared his feelings with me. To my surprise, he was interested and actively seeking a life partner. He had already spoken to our community leader and received approval for our relationship. This revelation marked the beginning of a new chapter in our lives.

We Started Dating

Our courtship began with a sense of clarity and excitement. We spent more time together, exploring our shared interests and deepening our connection. Our conversations grew more meaningful, and I looked forward to each interaction with anticipation.

Our first official date was at a charming diner, where he shared his thoughts with me. I responded by saying, "It's about time." The meal was delightful, and we spent hours talking about our dreams, goals, and values. I was thrilled to see him open up and share his thoughts and aspirations. It was during these moments that I began to understand the depth of his character and the sincerity of his intentions.

Introducing him to my family was a significant step in our relationship. My mother was particularly impressed by his thoughtfulness. He brought flowers for her, a gesture that spoke volumes about his respect and consideration. It was a moment that cemented his place in my family's hearts.

We dated for fifteen months before getting engaged.

During this time, our relationship grew stronger. We navigated the complexities of intimacy and communication, facing challenges and celebrating successes together. His commitment to purity before marriage was a value I respected, though it also brought challenges to our physical relationship.

Our conversations about intimacy were often difficult. His hesitation and discomfort with physical affection were puzzling, and I struggled with feelings of rejection. I had hoped for a more open dialogue about our needs and desires, but these discussions often left me feeling frustrated and uncertain.

As we approached the engagement stage, I was eager to move forward but anxious about the future. Our discussions about marriage and commitment often felt superficial. I wanted to ensure we were both prepared for the lifelong journey ahead. Despite my frustrations, I remained steadfast in my belief that our relationship was meant to be.

The Engagement and Wedding

Our engagement came on February 12, and a snowstorm threatened to derail our plans. My mom, aware of the event, had to convince me to leave my home that day, and she drove me there. The day seemed destined for romance, and the proposal went off without a hitch despite the challenging weather. He had orchestrated a beautiful setting with roses and a proposal sign, and the moment was nothing short of magical. I was overwhelmed with joy and gratitude.

We began planning our wedding with enthusiasm. The process was filled with excitement and anticipation, and our big day became a celebration of our love and commitment. Surrounded by friends and family, we exchanged vows and embarked on our journey as husband and wife.

The Honeymoon

Our honeymoon was a time of mixed emotions. I had anticipated it as the culmination of our waiting, but his hesitation and lack of eagerness dampened my enthusiasm. While we shared some memorable experiences, there was an underlying sense of disconnection in our intimacy.

We explored new places and created lasting memories, but the lack of physical closeness was disheartening. I began to question whether this was a temporary phase or a sign of deeper issues. My past experiences and expectations shaped my perspective, and I struggled to reconcile the gap between my desires and his responses.

Our conversations about intimacy were often avoided, and his frequent refrain that "there's a right time for everything" became a source of frustration. I felt that our marriage was being overshadowed by unspoken issues and unmet needs. The honeymoon phase, which I had hoped would be a time of joy and connection, instead became a period of introspection and uncertainty.

As we navigated our early days of marriage, I realized how important it is to address hidden struggles and addictions before committing to a lifetime together. Transparency about challenges and a willingness to confront difficult topics are essential for building a strong and fulfilling relationship.

Our journey was just beginning, and I knew that understanding and addressing these issues would be crucial to establishing a strong and lasting bond. It was a time of growth, both individually and as a couple, and I was committed to working through our challenges with patience and faith.

CHAPTER 2:

The Truth He Didn't Tell Me

The honeymoon was over, and it was time to start our real lives. It's funny how people talk about the honeymoon phase like it's some sort of fairy tale, where everything is perfect and magical. But no one warns you about what happens when the magic fades and reality sets in. That was when I began to notice something unsettling about my husband: he had a habit—a pattern, almost—of making decisions that affected us both without ever consulting me. Decisions I would have thought were ours to make together. Was this his idea of leadership? To decide without discussion? To lead without consideration? I couldn't help but think, this can't be right. This wasn't what I signed up for.

We had agreed—or at least, I thought we had—that I would leave my mother's home and move into his apartment after the wedding. It was part of the plan, part of the new life we were supposed to start together. But imagine my shock when I found out that, behind my back, he had gone to my mother and asked if he could move in with us instead. Us. As in, me and my mother. What? I was blindsided. He knew I would have objected; that's why he didn't tell me. That's why he went behind my back and excluded me from the decision entirely. And my mother, God bless her, agreed without even realizing I was out of the loop. It was as if I didn't exist in my own life.

When I found out, I was beyond distraught. I was heartbroken, betrayed by the man to whom I had just pledged my life. How could they make this decision without me? Was the reason financial? Did he think her home was better because it had more space? Or, more disturbingly, was he hiding something, maybe trying to avoid running into ghosts from his past—people I didn't know about? The questions kept swirling in my mind, but no answers came. I was left with a profound sense of unease, living in a situation I hadn't chosen, and all I could do was try to move forward.

And forward we moved—or at least pretended to. We returned to our community, our friends, our family, and I had to plaster a smile on my face. After all, we had just returned from our honeymoon; what could possibly be wrong? But behind that smile, the pretending began. Pretending that everything was fine, that we were happy, that this was what marriage was supposed to be. My husband didn't open the door for the deep conversations I desperately needed. There was never a good time to talk, to ask why, to express how hurt I was. He always seemed so easily disturbed, so irritable when I brought up anything remotely serious. What kind of spirit was at work in him that made me feel like I was the problem? Was it pride? Control? I couldn't figure it out. All I knew was that I was growing increasingly isolated in my own marriage.

The isolation was painful, especially because I saw him with others, his friends. With them, he could talk for hours, day or night. I envied them. I envied that they got the time, the attention, and the care that I longed for. I brought this to his attention more than once, but there was always an excuse. Always a reason why he couldn't give me the same time, the same attention. As the days turned into months, nothing changed. I did the only thing I knew how to do: I prayed. I prayed with all my heart, asking, God, where are you? I was sure, absolutely sure, that God had sent this man to me. He had placed an unusual love for him in my heart, a love that persisted even through the pain. I truly loved and cared for him, but it seemed like that love wasn't enough.

My Competition

Over time, I realized that my husband's attention was drifting elsewhere. I was no longer his priority, and it became painfully clear that I had competition.

1. The Bible

Yes, you read that right. The Bible became my first—and perhaps most formidable—competitor. My husband was a man of God; he often taught the Word, and that was one of the qualities I admired most about him. But our marriage wasn't what I had envisioned. We lacked the kind of emotional connection newly married couples should share. I've always been an affectionate woman, the kind who loves to be close, to touch, to connect. But he didn't know how to receive that. Worse, he rejected it. I felt rejected.

I'm a beautiful, intelligent, confident woman. I'm well-dressed, well-maintained, and I worship God with all my heart—the very qualities he said he wanted in a wife. So why couldn't I get his attention? What did I have to do? I began to suspect that my confidence and high self-esteem made him uncomfortable because he doubted himself. And so, inevitably, I started to back off. I began to withdraw, to stop trying so hard. But it hurt. It hurt deeply.

Night after night, when it was time for bed, my husband would tell me he had to study, that the quiet of the night was his favorite time to write. I understood and respected that. After all, the Bible does tell us to study to show ourselves approved. But didn't the Bible also say to lay with your wife? To cherish her? I knew that his nightly studies weren't just about the Word—they were about avoidance. And how do you compete with the Bible? I spent many nights alone, hurting, yet feeling the need to be strong, to protect his manhood, to pretend that I was okay with it all.

2. The Park

During the day, my competition wasn't the Bible— it was the park. My husband loved the park. He would leave early in the morning while I was still in bed, slipping out quietly to spend time alone. I often asked to go with him, to share that space, that time, but he'd tell me he needed to be alone. I respected that; everyone needs time to themselves. But it hurt. I loved the park too. I loved walking and spending time in nature, and I suggested we take a blanket and some snacks to spend the day there together. But he wasn't interested. He would resist and push back, as if the idea of spending time with me in the park was somehow burdensome.

The strange thing was, he would later tell me he wanted me to be more affectionate. Affectionate? How could he say that when every time I offered it, he turned me away? I started to wonder if this was his way of deflecting from the truth, of making me feel like the problem was me when, in reality, he was the one pulling away. I suggested we take different routes on our walks, but he always had to be in control. It was always his way, never mine. And it made me question everything. Was he hiding something? Was there a reason he didn't want to spend time with me, specifically?

3. His Friends

And then there were his friends—another competition. My husband always made sure he didn't miss a call or a text from them, no matter the time, no matter the place. Being there for them seemed to give him value, a sense of purpose that I couldn't compete with. He was a wise man with excellent counseling skills, and people sought him out for advice, comfort, and support. They would often approach us, sharing how much his words had helped them, how grateful they were for his guidance. Hearing them speak so highly of him always made me proud. He truly was a great man. But there was a price to be paid for that greatness, and it seemed that I was the one paying it.

They needed him, and he was there for them— always. I, on the other hand, had to wait. I had to be patient, understanding, and accepting of the fact that I wasn't his priority. I had to remind myself, time and again, that this was who he was: a man of God, a man of the people, someone who was there for others. But in doing so, I lost sight of who I was and what I needed.

This continued for years, and eventually, I became comfortable with it—or at least I told myself I was. But then, something shifted. His friends started getting married, and they now had wives to attend to. Suddenly, the dynamics changed. He tried to make me understand that he had been this way long before we met, that his commitment to his friends was just part of who he was. But I expected more. I expected him to prioritize me, to put our marriage first. And maybe that was selfish of me, but it was how I felt.

At the time, I didn't fully understand his emotional needs or how they manifested in his actions. But that didn't make it any easier to accept. I felt neglected and pushed aside, and as much as I tried to understand and be patient, the resentment started to build. I couldn't help but wonder: where do I fit in?

The Counseling Session

The breaking point came one day when I couldn't take it anymore. I wrote him an angry letter. I needed to express my pain, to let out all the hurt and frustration I'd been holding inside. I poured it all out on the page: my suspicions, my fears, my heartbreak over how our honeymoon had been anything but. I wrote the words that had been gnawing at me: "That was not a honeymoon." I knew those words would cut deep, but they were my truth. And I was desperate to be heard. He didn't like what I had to say—not one bit. And instead of coming to me, instead of talking it out, he went straight to our leader with the letter without telling me. Yet again, he decided without me. And so, we were called into our leader's office to discuss what I had written and to receive counseling.

When I wrote that letter, it had been six weeks since we last had sex. I accused him of certain things, things I couldn't prove but felt deeply. His actions and his behavior all pointed to something being wrong, and I couldn't shake the feeling that there was more to the story than he was telling me. During our session, he denied it all. He turned the focus on me—on my lack of domestic effort, on how he felt unloved and uncared for. I couldn't argue with that; there was truth in what he said. I hadn't been the perfect wife. I had been unmotivated and distant, and it showed. But his words still stung. I felt like I was being blamed for everything, as if my feelings didn't matter.

I cried during that meeting. It was the first time I let myself be vulnerable in front of someone else, and it was painful. One of the things my husband said during the session was that he deserved to be loved. Deserved? I looked at him, stunned. Did he really just say that? Did he think I didn't deserve to be loved too? That I didn't deserve to feel cherished, valued, and cared for? I was furious. I wanted to scream, to hit him, to make him understand how much he was hurting me. But at the same time, I felt a deep sadness for him. Maybe he didn't feel loved, and that's why he didn't know how to give it. Hurt people hurt people, right?

Our leader tried to mediate, to offer us words of wisdom. I could see he was tired, and I wondered how much of what we were saying was really getting through. But I knew I couldn't blame him for not understanding the full picture; I hadn't told him everything. Even in that moment, I was still protecting my husband, still trying to preserve his image. I couldn't bring myself to tell the whole truth, to reveal the depth of my pain. And so, the cycle continued. I left that session feeling a mix of relief and despair. Relief that I had finally spoken up, but despair that nothing had really changed. I always thought we would have had an almost perfect marriage if not for his struggle because he is a great man.

The Ride Home

As we left our leader's office, we were instructed to hug. And of course, I wanted to hug my husband. Despite everything, I loved him and wanted the best for us. I could tell he felt the same, even if he couldn't always show it. That hug gave me a glimmer of hope. Maybe, just maybe, this was the turning point. Maybe things would get better now that everything was out in the open.

We didn't say much on the ride home, but my mind was racing. I felt a strange sense of peace, a quiet confidence that things were about to change for the better. I had prayed for this, and now it seemed like my prayers were being answered. I was hopeful, optimistic, and ready to move forward. For a while, things did improve. I could see him trying—trying to please me, to be more attentive. And I appreciated it; I really did. But it didn't feel natural. It felt forced, as if he was doing it out of obligation rather than genuine desire. It was like a tug-of-war, both of us struggling to get it right but never quite succeeding.

As time passed, the old patterns crept back in. The same issues resurfaced, and we were right back where we started.

One of the biggest challenges was communication—or rather, the lack of it. Whenever I tried to express my concerns, he would turn the conversation around, pointing out my flaws and my shortcomings. And just like that, I would shut down. It felt almost abusive, the way he deflected and made me feel like the problem was always me. And so, we never resolved anything. We never got to the root of our issues.

He interpreted any criticism as an attack, becoming defensive and shutting down. I didn't understand how to communicate in a way that he could receive, and I didn't know how to help him with whatever he was dealing with. It was like we were speaking different languages, and the more I tried to reach out, the more he pulled away.

Despite everything, I never lost my sense of self- worth. I knew I wasn't the problem. I knew I wasn't his preference, but that didn't diminish my value as a woman. I held on to what God said about me, and no one—not even my husband—could take that away. My inner resolve kept me going, even though I was tired, drained, and desperate for a mental break.

But if you think that was enough to break me, just wait for the next chapter.

CHAPTER 3:

The Call

A Day I'll Never Forget

Imagine this: you're at work, having a good day. Everything feels normal, like any other day. You have your routine, your tasks, and your plans for when you get home. But little do you know; this is the day your life will change forever. This is the day when everything you thought you knew about your life, your marriage, and your future would be turned upside down.

Now, I know some of you reading this may not believe in God, but I do. And after everything I'd already been through, I clung to the belief that God wouldn't allow me to bear more than I could handle. That's what they say in church, right? "God won't give you more than you can bear." But if that's true, God must have had a lot of faith in me, because more did come, so much more, and I wasn't ready for any of it. Not even close.

It all started with a call. The kind of call that stops you in your tracks. The kind of call that makes your heart race and your mind spin, wondering what could be so important that it couldn't wait until you got home. Why did I have to leave work early? What could be so urgent? I've always been the type to keep calm under pressure, to stay composed even in the most frightening situations, but this felt different. It felt like something was about to happen that would change everything.

It was early in the afternoon when the call came from our leader. He asked if I could come to his home at 4 PM and mentioned that my husband would be there too. The way he spoke, carefully choosing his words, told me everything I needed to know this was serious. This was something big. I could hear the effort in his voice, the way he was trying to stay calm and not alarm me. But I was already alarmed, how could I not be? By this point, my husband and I had only been married for seventeen months. It wasn't long, but it was long enough for me to know when something was very, very wrong.

As soon as I hung up, I wanted time to speed up and slow down all at once. My heart was racing, and I couldn't focus on work anymore. All I could think about was what this could mean. I wasn't supposed to leave work until 5 PM, so I had to ask my supervisor if I could leave early, claiming there was an emergency at home. And there was— though I didn't know exactly what it was yet. She gave me the go-ahead, and I left, heading to the train that would take me to our leader's home.

That train ride was the most uncomfortable, most terrifying journey I'd ever taken. It felt like an eternity, and with every passing second, my anxiety grew. My mind raced with questions. Did someone die? Was someone in the hospital? Was I accused of something? Was my husband asking for a divorce? Did he regret marrying me? And if that were the case, why would he go to our leader before coming to me? Then again, based on past experiences, that wouldn't have surprised me, he had previously made critical marital decisions without me. As I sat there, staring out the window but not really seeing anything, I tried to find a glimmer of hope. I told myself that everything would be okay, that maybe this wasn't as bad as it seemed. But optimism just wouldn't come. No matter how hard I tried, I couldn't shake the feeling that my worst fears were about to come true. This woman of faith, this woman who always tried to see the good in every situation, couldn't find a single positive thought. I started taking deep breaths, trying to calm myself and remind myself that worrying wouldn't help. But it was no use. I was scared. I was more scared than I'd ever been in my life.

I kept telling myself that whatever was waiting for me, I would get through it. I'd come this far, and I had so much further to go. After all, the prophetic words spoken over my life hadn't yet come to pass. But as much as I thought about it, I wasn't sure I believed it. Not really. Not in that moment.

The Reveal:

When I finally arrived at our leader's home, he and another leader greeted me. And there he was—my husband. He was sitting there with a look that I can only describe as a mixture of sadness and fear. Or maybe that's just how I interpreted it. My leader asked if I was okay, and I said yes, but the truth was, I was far from okay. I was barely holding it together.

Then he started to speak. My husband remained silent, just sitting there, not saying a word. I knew right then that they had discussed this before I arrived. They had planned who would break the news to me and how it would be done to make it easier on my husband. And then the words came out, words that would change everything: My husband had confessed to our leader that he had been struggling with sexual attraction to men.

There it was—the truth. The truth he hadn't told me.

Now, I know you saw that one coming. I won't pretend I was shocked because, deep down, I had known. I had even accused him of it in the letter I wrote. But hearing it out loud, hearing it confirmed by someone else—that was different. That was real. That was my life, my marriage, falling apart right before me. I felt like stitches were being given to me all over my body without anesthesia.

I sat there, listening, my heart pounding so hard I thought it might burst out of my chest. But I didn't cry. I didn't break down. I just sat there, letting it all sink in. There was more to come. It wasn't just a simple confession. It wasn't just something he had decided to share one day. No, there was a reason for it—a catalyst that had forced him to come clean.

He had found himself in a situation where he desired to have sex with a man, and the opportunity was there. He didn't go through with it, but the man he was with had told a family member. My husband knew that it was only a matter of time before this became public knowledge. He understood what could happen if word got out. He recognized the serious ramifications, not just for him, but for us, for our marriage, for everything we had built. It is only by God's grace that, to this day, this man is still one of our dearest and closest family friends, happily married and doing amazing things. Only God can do this!

The most painful part of all this was hearing that it happened in our home. Our home was the place where we were supposed to be safe, where we were supposed to build a life together—the place where I felt disrespected in the worst way possible. What was he thinking? How could he do this to me? To us?

But even at that moment, I didn't cry. I didn't scream. I didn't throw anything or break down hysterically. I just sat there, feeling numb. It was like everything was happening to someone else, not to me. This was my marriage we were talking about—my life—but I felt detached, like I was watching it all unfold from a distance. It was as if showing that I was strong was my badge of honor.

This was not just a bump in the road. This was a mountain, a total roadblock, with no way around it. It was dark, and I couldn't see the other side. I couldn't see the light at the end of the tunnel, and I had no idea where to step next. Good marriages require hard work, but this? This was something else entirely. This was abnormal. This was a test of my commitment, my love for my husband, and my faith in God.

Our leader, trying to manage the situation, asked me to call the family member who knew what had happened. He wanted me to get a feel for what was going on on their side—to assess the damage, so to speak. I remember thinking how inconsiderate and insensitive that was. How could he ask me to get on the phone minutes after finding out about my husband and talk to this person? I couldn't bring myself to do it, even though he persisted. What was I supposed to say? How was I supposed to act? And all the while, inside, I was terrified, ashamed, and overwhelmed.

It didn't take long for me to realize that our leader's priority was damage control for the church. My feelings, my pain, and my marriage were secondary. The church had to be protected. The church had to come first.

Going Home Again:

The ride home was silent. It was like we were two strangers sitting next to each other, no one knowing what to say. I was numb—completely numb. We had only been living in our apartment for two months and married for seventeen months. And yet, it felt like a lifetime of loneliness had been packed into that short time.

Now, there was no more denying it. We both had to face the truth. He had justified my ominous feelings, the suspicions that had kept me up at night. There was no more pretending, no more brushing things under the rug. I had to deal with this quiet chaos inside me. I felt like I was in a nightmare, and I couldn't wake up.

There were so many questions swirling in my mind: How could he do this to me? How could he keep this from me? Why didn't he tell me about his struggle before we got married? It was a betrayal of the worst kind. And how was I supposed to trust him again? How could I forgive him enough even to try? Where do we go from here? Was this the end of our marriage? How was I supposed to tell my mother? How would she react? What would people think about divorce after such a short time of being married? How would we face our community? I knew it wouldn't take long for the word to get out, and then what?

As all these questions raced through my mind, we returned home. My husband didn't know what to say to me, and I didn't know what to say to him. What could he possibly say? "I'm sorry?" Those words wouldn't mean anything to me right now. I could see the shame all over him, and once again, I felt bad for him, forgetting about myself. Of course, he continued coming to bed after I'd fallen asleep, avoiding me, avoiding confrontation. It made no sense for him to pretend now, but still, he did.

I had so many questions, but I didn't ask them. There was no yelling, no screaming. We remained cordial with each other, almost as if we were just roommates going through the motions.

The Next Few Days:

Our leader advised us to stay at my mother's home for a while, out of the public eye, while they deliberated on the best course of action. Once again, I wasn't included in the decision-making process that would affect my marriage.

Everything was being handled for me, as if I were a child who couldn't be trusted with her own life.

Don't get me wrong—I'm not saying our leaders didn't mean well. I know they believed they were doing what was best to defuse a potentially explosive situation. They were trying to protect the church, and I understood that. But what about me? Where was the consideration for me—the one who had been wronged, the one left to pick up the pieces? I was the casualty of my husband's actions, yet he got all the attention. He was the one being protected, while I had to stand back and watch it all unfold.

They decided my husband would leave for a while to remove him from the situation, giving him time to "heal" and figure things out. There were moments when I felt that some in the church would have been relieved if I'd chosen to divorce him—because that would sever his connection to the church.

I had just discovered my husband's struggle, and we hadn't even had a real conversation about it. There was no counseling before he left, no attempt to help us work through this together. It was simply, "He's going away, and that's that." My world had been turned upside down, and I was left alone with nothing but confusion, sadness, and exhaustion.

He was gone within days. I remember the day he left— it was New Year's Eve. We would have celebrated the New Year together if he had stayed, but instead, I was alone. He wasn't there to kiss at midnight or to hold me as we watched other couples celebrating. But I didn't miss a beat. I went to church that night and lifted my hands in worship as if nothing had happened. The person leading worship knew what I was going through, and I could see the amazement in her eyes when she saw me.

The next day, I returned alone to our apartment. I had no idea what the future held, but I was determined to believe there was purpose in my pain. I had to accept that— had to believe it.

Returning to Work

New Year's Day was a holiday, giving me one day to rest and process everything before returning to work. I had a perfectly good reason to stay home the next day, to take some time for myself. But did I stay home? Of course not. I got up, got dressed as usual, and arrived at work early.

That morning, the train ride felt different. I was a woman who had woken up alone—no husband to see, no goodbye kiss. It was a sad day, and I felt the tears rising inside me, but I held them back. A still, quiet voice whispered that everything would be alright. I clung to that voice, that flicker of reassurance, even though I didn't fully believe it.

Staying focused at work was difficult. My supervisor knew both my husband and me well; we were part of the same circles. I couldn't bring myself to explain what had happened, but I did tell her that my husband was away for a while. She asked why, and I just said, "I can't tell you, but I'm sure you'll hear about it." And she did.

That day felt like one of the longest I'd ever experienced at work. I couldn't wait to get home, eager to talk to my husband. I had so many questions—so many things I needed to understand—but I knew that day might not be the right time to ask.

Even in the middle of my own emotional distress, I couldn't stop thinking about what my husband must be feeling. After all, this was his shame, his struggle. He had to face his family, who I knew would fully support him. But

I also knew one of his greatest fears was whether I would leave him now. The loneliness he must have felt inside was probably even greater than mine.

There were so many unanswered questions. How would we handle our sexual desires now? Would I find myself tempted to run into the arms of another man for comfort? Would he give in to desires for men or women while he was away? And then there were practical concerns—how would we maintain financial stability now that one income was gone? There was so much to process, and I didn't have all the answers.

Settling in Alone

I tried not to let the stress overwhelm me, so I focused on self-care—eating well, exercising, and sticking to a routine. It wasn't always easy, but I knew it was important, especially now. It would have been so easy to slip into depression, to let the weight of everything crush me. But I couldn't let that happen. I had to keep going, had to maintain appearances, had to keep smiling for everyone to see.

I didn't open up to anyone in depth about what was happening. I couldn't. The few people who knew didn't know how to approach me or what to say. My support network was minimal, and though I knew I needed therapy, I wasn't ready to share such personal, sensitive information with anyone. And no one insisted on it.

I had to accept that it was okay to feel hurt and angry. But honestly, I'm not sure I ever fully accepted that. I'm not sure I ever truly allowed myself to grieve. Instead, I spent a lot of time alone thinking, processing, and trying to make sense of everything.

But God was good to me. Every morning, I woke up with a song in my heart. Songs I hadn't heard in a long time would just come to me, comforting me, lifting me up. The Holy Spirit was my helper, my comforter, and my constant companion through it all.

Keeping in Touch:

Even though we were miles apart, my husband and I communicated daily. He needed to know that he had my full support, and I needed to remind him that I was still here, still committed to our marriage. I visited him as often as I could, though it became an expensive habit after a while.

Once, while planning a trip to see him, a family member

asked why I was spending my money that way. I had to remind her that he was still my husband. This came from someone who had never been married, so I didn't expect her to understand. But I knew what I was doing. I knew I had to keep fighting for my marriage, no matter what.

The first time I visited, I didn't tell him I was coming. A family member picked me up and drove me to the house where he was staying. I remember seeing him standing on the porch as we pulled up—his smile and the joy on his face were priceless. It was a good visit, but leaving was tough. As you'd imagine, it was very emotional, and I cried the entire trip back.

One day, I tried calling my husband, but I couldn't reach him. Panic set in. I called his family, but they just said he was out.

"Out?" I thought to myself. *"This is not the time to be out of touch for an entire day."* I wanted to visit him again, but he insisted I shouldn't, and I couldn't understand why.

Later that night, my doorbell rang. When I opened the door, there he was, surprising me with an unexpected visit. A friend of ours had picked him up and brought him home.

It was an emotional, fun night, but it was also the first time I saw him cry. That night, he opened up about the shame he felt—the weight of disappointing those who loved him. He stayed with me for a few days before returning to where he'd been staying.

It was frustrating at times. I wanted to ask him the tough questions—the ones I desperately needed answers to. But whenever I tried to engage him in a deep conversation, he became agitated. He wasn't ready to face the reality of what had happened.

"I don't want to think about that now," he'd say.

So, I didn't press him. I told myself he just needed time, that he'd eventually open up, and we'd have that conversation. But it never happened—not while we were apart.

What I'm Learning

At this point, I learned that when life gives you lemons, you have to make lemonade. Love can be challenging, especially when you're apart, and I knew I had to build resilience to keep going. I needed to channel my emotions into spiritual growth. We all make mistakes, so I had to do some introspection. Could I have done something differently? Could

I have helped him trust me enough to share his struggle? Was there something I was doing that made him feel unsafe? I knew that sex is important in a healthy marriage, but I also learned that I could still love my husband without it while we worked on rebuilding our relationship—and I did love him, deeply.

I had to take it one day at a time because the future was uncertain. The pain was real, and there was a lot of it, but I was determined not to let it turn into suffering. I reminded myself that my circumstances didn't define my worth—I did. My self-worth came from within, from what God said about me. I was confident before I met my husband, and that hadn't changed. If I hadn't been sure of who I was—if I hadn't carried that inner resolve—things could have turned out very differently. I might have become bitter and resentful. But I refused to let that happen.

To all men and women: Don't let another person or a marriage define your worth. If you do, when your spouse fails you, it can leave permanent scars, leading to bitterness and unforgiveness. Love yourself first so you can give that love to someone else. You can't share love with someone if you don't have it for yourself.

CHAPTER 4:

Who Am I?

By now, you might be thinking that I'm some young, naive, weak, or inexperienced person with no voice of her own. Let me stop you right there. That assumption couldn't be further from the truth. So, let me take a moment to enlighten you about who I really am.

When I met my now-husband, I had already been through the wringer. I had been previously married, divorced, and was raising a twelve-year-old child on my own. Yes, I was a single mother, navigating the complexities that come with that territory for at least nine years. I wasn't fresh out of some fairy tale or stepping into marriage without a clue. I had already lived through the ups and downs of a relationship, and I knew a thing or two about life.

Let's rewind a bit. I married my first husband at a young age—too young, if I'm being honest. Back then, I didn't know God, and I certainly didn't know how to be a good wife or what it took to build a healthy marriage. I didn't have role models or examples in my family to guide me. Most of the women in my family were single, so there was no one to pull me aside and say, "You're too young. Wait a few years. You've got your whole life ahead of you. Take your time to really know him."

But we were young and in love—or at least, we thought we were. My first husband was a good man, and we were both just figuring things out as we went. We were married and lived together for a few years before everything started to fall apart. I remember those early days, being head over heels in love and wanting to spend every waking moment with him. We lived in different counties, which meant a lot of traveling back and forth, often on late-night train rides, since neither of us owned a car.

Here's the thing, though: as much as I wanted to be with him, I also felt a certain pressure to get married when we did. He didn't have his immigration status, so there was this sense of urgency on his part. And on my end, there was a feeling of guilt, which made me rush into the marriage without fully thinking it through. Looking back now, I see how young and unprepared we both were.

The biggest challenge in our marriage was that I loved to socialize and have fun with my friends. I was young and full of life, and I wanted to be out, dancing, laughing, and enjoying myself. My then-husband, on the other hand, was a workaholic. He would work late evenings and weekends, and while he was working, I was out with my friends, partying and attending every event possible. I was married, but I still had a very single- minded way of thinking. And as you can imagine, having your wife out partying while you're working doesn't sit well with any man.

To make matters worse, I was incredibly independent. I didn't rely on him for much, which only added to the strain on our relationship. Over time, the arguments became more heated, especially on his side. Eventually, the emotional abuse began—degrading comments that slowly chipped away at my self-esteem. We didn't know how to communicate in a way that allowed us to understand each other's needs and feelings. And because we kept everything to ourselves, there was no help, no intervention to save our marriage.

There was no infidelity, no addictions, and no physical abuse—just two young people who didn't know how to make it work. I vividly remember one day when our toddler was in the bedroom with us, and my then- husband, in a moment of anger, said something harsh to me. As I looked at our child's innocent face, a realization hit me: I couldn't let this continue. I didn't know how to pray, fast, or believe that God could change us. I just knew I didn't want to raise my child in a toxic environment.

When I asked him to leave, he was shocked and deeply hurt. He hadn't seen it coming, and neither had our families, since no one knew what we were dealing with behind closed doors. But he left quietly, without much resistance.

I've never regretted that decision. It was the right choice for both of us, and I've always been grateful for the lessons I learned from that marriage. Those lessons made me a better wife the second time around. Most importantly, I am blessed with an extraordinary child— kind, thoughtful, brilliant, and wise beyond his years. If you ever meet my child, you'll understand exactly what I mean.

The Accounting Clerk:

I've always had a natural affinity for numbers. Math came easily to me throughout my school years, and I was one of those kids who could do complex calculations in my head without breaking a sweat. It amazed people. They'd watch me solve a problem and ask, "How did you do that?"

In college, I majored in Business Management and Finance, so it was no surprise that I gravitated toward positions in accounting departments. After graduation, my first job was in the accounting department of a printing company. My duties covered everything related to accounting and payroll. With minimal training, I caught on quickly and excelled at the job. I took pride in my work and was the kind of person who wouldn't stop searching until I found that missing penny. I took ownership of my responsibilities.

It was during that first job that the desire to open my own business began to take root. I remember watching my boss leave the office every day at lunchtime, only to return with bags of clothes from her shopping trips. Day after day, I observed this, and each time, my desire to be in her position grew stronger. I wanted to be the one who could leave my employees, go shopping, and come back with bags full of goodies. That's when I started researching business ideas—the seed had been planted.

I spent a few years at that company, and as I gained more experience, I moved on to other positions in other companies, each time with a higher income. But at that young age, I wasn't yet a good steward of my finances. I spent as much as I earned—and sometimes more.

My next position was at a major clothing store, one you would probably recognize if I mentioned the name. And, of course, they offered that tempting employee discount. Guess what I did? Every Friday, I went shopping, used my discount, and gave part of my paycheck right back to the store. If only I had taken my mother's advice and saved my money, I would have accomplished so much more at a younger age.

"I went through my adult years without much interruption in employment.". I interviewed well, had a pleasant personality, and, as one employer once told me, I was "fair to look upon." Let's not forget that I was also intelligent. With each new position, I learned more, took on more responsibilities—and, yes, spent more money. But after a while, I would always feel a sense of unease. Something inside me kept whispering, "Don't settle. Go after your dreams."

I knew deep down that a 9-to-5 job wasn't for me. I craved the freedom and flexibility to pursue my passions and do other things that truly fulfilled me. The corporate world felt like a trap, but that didn't stop me from giving my best. If anything, it motivated me to work harder and strive for more.

In every office I worked in, I was the cool cucumber—the one who kept the peace among employees.

When coworkers came to me with complaints, I encouraged them to talk directly to each other rather than vent to me. Can you believe that? It always seemed easier to give advice when you weren't the one living through the situation.

I've always had the heart of a peacemaker, and that tendency carried over into my marriage—but not in the healthiest way. I realized I needed to learn how to speak up and assert myself so I could find inner peace, not just keep external peace for everyone else.

Business Owner:

Despite the challenges, I managed to achieve something that not everyone does: I became a business owner. I was a college-educated woman operating her own business while simultaneously holding down a 9-to-5 job. But let me tell you, achieving this didn't come without its hurdles. It took multiple tries and failures before I finally got my business off the ground. But I didn't give up. I was determined. I was both the boss of my employees and an employee of someone else's company. I found immense joy in being able to provide jobs to people I knew.

Of course, being the boss wasn't always easy. There were times when I had to make tough decisions, whether it was providing constructive feedback or, in some cases, letting someone go. But I handled it with maturity and grace. Every day, I would leave one job and go to the other, juggling the demands of clients for my employer and clients for my own business. As you can imagine, it takes a strong, mentally and emotionally resilient person to do that successfully—and I did it.

This experience taught me a lot. It helped me understand my employees' needs because I was one of them. It also gave me insight into what my bosses had to deal with and what they expected, since I was a boss too. Overall, I became a more valuable employee and a better employer. Of course, I didn't always get it right—none of us do—but I was committed to learning, growing, and improving as a person.

Now, more than twenty years later, I'm still running my own business. It's in my blood. I'm wired for this, and I enjoy it immensely. When my husband met me, he didn't find a weak, uncertain woman; he met a strong, financially stable, independent-minded, and happy woman who was enjoying life and had good things happening for her. I remember telling God that if He wanted to keep me single for the rest of my life, I was okay with that. I was content with who I was and the life I was living. And I meant it. But God had other plans for me.

As a child, I always felt I would be a wealthy woman—not just in terms of material possessions, but in having more than enough to help others. I admired the children around me whose parents were doctors and lawyers, who had more than I did, and I wanted that for myself. I've always loved traveling, and my financial status allowed me to do so. I was able to enroll my child in a private school, which I paid for, and I could buy him whatever he wanted without any help. I found joy in giving generously and helping friends and family in need.

Financially Stable:

In my early twenties, I secured my first paid position and was able to maintain financial stability without interruption. I never depended on anyone outside of my mother, and I was blessed in that way. My life was stable in terms of finances; my expenses were always paid without worry, and I had extra funds for whatever I chose to do. Over time, I learned how to budget well and became more responsible with my money, which laid the foundation for building financial security.

I was always setting goals, both short-term and long- term. I didn't always meet my targets, but I never gave up on my aspirations. Maintaining a good credit score became a top priority because I knew it was one of the keys to success. I have always been interested in different forms of investment. Having multiple income streams and paying myself first was important, so I sought out passive income and investment opportunities. I spent hours on the internet searching for information and learning new things. I wasn't afraid to take risks with my investments, even though sometimes those risks didn't pay off.

Over the years, investors have presented me with many opportunities. If an investment made sense, I would give it a try. And with each failure, I learned a valuable lesson. I was motivated by the freedom to make choices that aligned with my values and goals. I took the saying, "There is no reward without risk," to heart. Some of those risks were calculated, and some were not. But I told myself, "I'll make that money back." I was the one people looked to for help, and I prided myself on that. I hardly ever experienced money-related stress. The financial security I felt gave me resilience in the face of emergencies and a sense of confidence.

This stability earned me a certain level of respect, but it also meant I had to be cautious. I had to avoid people without discretion who wanted to take advantage of my generosity.

Church Leadership Role

From the moment I committed to becoming a faithful church member, it didn't take long for me to start volunteering on a team in an administrative position. I grew up with a grandmother who was a great example of what it meant to serve. I watched her faithfully serve her community for as long as I can remember. She never said no when the opportunity arose to give her time and make a difference to those around her. Her loyalty and commitment were unmatched, and everyone loved her.

My grandmother instilled those same qualities in me, and I served with the same faithfulness and zeal, enjoying every moment. My responsibilities included planning events, registering members, collecting payments when necessary, and connecting with vendors to ensure everything would go smoothly. I enjoyed this work immensely, knowing that I was helping the church and the community. My organizational skills and attention to detail made my duties effortless.

I served in that capacity for many years, and over time, I took on additional responsibilities. I became involved in the youth ministry, working with other leaders to plan weekly activities for the youth. We organized Bible studies, social events, game nights, movie nights, and outdoor trips. Mentoring became an automatic part of our duties as we worked with teenagers and young adults, helping them navigate their challenges and questions.

As the years went by, I joined the finance team and served there for over seventeen years, eventually becoming one of the team leaders. During that time, I also became one of the chosen few who would care for our pastors. When visiting pastors came, I would be assigned to care for at least one of them. My responsibilities didn't stop there; I assisted with social media and was responsible for regular communication with members.

Ministry travel was also a part of my life before I met my husband. It was easy for me, first because I loved traveling, but more importantly, because I was part of a team making a difference in the lives of others. I traveled to places like Nigeria, Rwanda, South Africa, Swaziland, various states in the USA, and a few Caribbean islands. I could go on and on, but I think you get the picture. You have a pretty good idea of who I am and what I'm about.

Submission or Weakness:

So, you're probably shocked now that I've given you an insight into who I was when I met my husband. Are you wondering how I allowed myself to be in the kind of marriage I've described? I would be wondering the same thing if I were reading about someone else.

Here I was: an independent-thinking, emotionally mature woman; a business owner; a leader with excellent decision-making skills; a mother; well-traveled; and financially stable. Yet, somehow, I was grossly underestimated by those around me. How could anyone think that a weak, naive woman could have accomplished the things I did?

But that's just it—my husband didn't believe I could handle it if he told me about his struggles. He didn't involve me when he decided we would live with my mother after we got married. I wasn't part of the decision- making process when he and our leaders decided he should go away. I felt invisible to those around me.

Being underestimated can be traumatic. It can make a person question their identity if they're not mentally and emotionally strong. It didn't make sense because I thought I had proven my ability to handle life's difficulties. But then, why didn't I speak up? Why did I allow this to happen?

We are taught a principle in the Bible about wives submitting to their husbands. First, let me say that I'm not here to argue that point, nor am I about to make excuses for anything I may or may not have done. But the truth is, I didn't fully understand what submission meant at the time. I learned the true meaning of submission years into my marriage.

I did my best to live at peace with my husband by not being combative when faced with situations I didn't like. I remained quiet. I told myself that the best thing to do was pray, and so I prayed. But at some point, my peacemaking, calm, and cool demeanor was seen as a weakness.

I wasn't the typical woman who yelled and refused to speak to her husband for days when she was upset. In my marriage, there was no such thing as my husband sleeping on the couch. He told me before we were married that he would never do that, even if I wanted him to. He wasn't the argumentative type, and he often remained quiet, which made it easy for me to be silent as well. After all, I couldn't have a conversation by myself.

There were no slamming doors, no dirty looks, no insults. But even with all that, I knew something was wrong. I had feelings of not being heard, feelings of rejection, and deep sadness. Sometimes, I was tempted to believe I wasn't good enough for him, but I never let that thought linger for too long. I knew I was more than enough. And I believed that God had brought us together for a reason, that I was exactly what my husband needed at the time.

But I honestly didn't know my husband's true thoughts about me then. I later learned that submission didn't mean I couldn't express my feelings, that I couldn't voice my disapproval, or that I didn't have a say in decisions that affected us as a couple. I didn't have to appear weak to prove that I was a submissive wife.

The funny thing is that the same qualities I had—qualities that may have seemed weak to others—were the ones I later needed to carry us through our marriage for the next few years.

CHAPTER 5:

Why Did He Marry Me? Was It a Cover?

It's only natural to wonder why he married me. Why did he choose me? What was going on in his heart and mind? The truth is, I don't have all the answers, and I'm not sure I ever will. But when he finally revealed the truth to me—his struggle with same-sex attraction— my mind couldn't help but wonder: Was our marriage a cover? A way for him to hide from the world, from himself?

Certain social, professional, and family expectations weigh heavily on us, especially in the church community we were part of. A marriage, a heterosexual marriage, could be a perfect defense against the perceptions he didn't want others to have about him. Many people get married for that very reason, and it's still prevalent today. So, I couldn't help but ask myself: Did he think that being in a heterosexual marriage would somehow make him whole? Did he believe that by marrying me, he could silence the desires that troubled him? If that was the case, what he needed was God, not a wife.

In the world we lived in, particularly in the church, same-sex lifestyles were not accepted. They were seen as something that needed to be shunned, something that had no place among "good Christians." Let me clarify, though: my husband was also attracted to women and had been in heterosexual relationships before. But did he believe that by marrying me, he could somehow push aside those other desires? Did he think that I would be understanding, or did he hope that marriage would magically make those feelings disappear? And then there's the most painful question of all: Was it true love when we said, "I do?"

These questions haunted me, spinning around in my mind with no answers in sight. It was a time of deep confusion, a time when everything I thought I knew about love, marriage, and faith was suddenly called into question. And the worst part? No one could help me answer these lingering doubts. Everything he said, everything he did, was now shrouded in uncertainty. How long could we keep this up before our marriage inevitably failed?

I believed in God's ability to transform minds and hearts, but the real question was: Did my husband want to be transformed? Was this something we could simply pray away, or was it something more complex, something that required more than just faith? This was my first time being so close to someone who struggled with same-sex desires, and I couldn't help but feel deeply empathetic. I didn't want to add to his isolation, and I certainly didn't want him to feel even more alienated by me or by those around him. What he needed was help, understanding, patience, and love. And yet, here I was again, focusing on what he needed while forgetting about my own needs.

It was so easy for those around us to jump to conclusions, to pass judgment, to say things like, "That could never be me." But in moments like these, I realized just how our Christian sexual ethics could close our eyes and hearts to those struggling with same-sex attractions. It made us cold, distant, and self-righteous. We loved from a distance because we didn't want to be associated with something we deemed unnatural. The stigma was too great. How could he be involved in such acts and still be a Christian? Did we ever stop to ask the right questions? Did anyone take the time to listen? Or did we just assume that the reasons didn't matter?

Why wasn't he comfortable going to someone for help? Was it because he saw our insensitive and judgmental attitudes toward that lifestyle? Or was it because he feared our reactions, feared that we would tell him to just stop, as if it were that simple? There were so many questions and so much uncertainty surrounding this matter, and no one had any immediate answers.

As I reflect on all of this, I want to encourage those who might be struggling with similar desires. The Bible says, "Let us also lay aside every encumbrance and the sin that so easily entangles us, and let us run with endurance the race that is set before us, fixing our eyes on Jesus, the author and perfecter of faith, who for the joy set before him endured the cross, despising the shame, and has sat down at the right hand of the throne of God" (Hebrews 12:1–2).

I remember one day when I was complaining to a wise friend about something my husband had done that upset me. It wasn't necessarily that he did something wrong; I just thought he could have done it differently. This friend, who was also married and had years of experience, listened patiently. I admired how she cared for her husband, and I trusted her advice. After I finished venting, she looked at me and said, "See him through the eyes of God."

It was excellent advice, but at the time, I was very much in my flesh. I remember thinking, who's seeing me? Why do I need to be the one to see him? He's the man; I needed him to see me. But those words of wisdom stuck with me. They lingered in my mind, even as I struggled with my feelings.

Was It Love?

He said he loved me, and I believed him. There were so many signs, so many gestures that seemed to prove his love. There was the engagement ceremony, which was like a mini wedding, filled with romance and sweet promises. He was great with words, and when he wanted to, he could be incredibly romantic. I would come home to find beautiful clothes laid out on the bed clothes he had bought for me just because. He had excellent taste in everything, and he took pleasure in surprising me.

The names he had for me on his phone were endearing. When we are home together, I would call his phone to see those sweet names flash on his screen. On the screen. My pictures were always his screensaver and wallpaper on both his phone and computer. He loved to cook, and he showed his love by serving my meals first, always with a smile. He would watch me eat, waiting for me to tell him how much I enjoyed the food. It became a running joke between us; he'd say, "Eat all," and we'd laugh.

He would occasionally tell his friends how much I meant to him and how grateful he was to have me in his life. He also shared some of the conversations he had with others about me. Random hugs and kisses were a regular part of our life together. He would reach for my hand when we were walking or driving, and if I hadn't touched him in a while, he'd let me know because it was important to him.

We talked about our long-term goals and our dreams for the future, and those conversations always showed his commitment to our marriage. He was always excited about traveling with me; travel was something we both loved, and we looked forward to those adventures together. He never failed to tell me how beautiful I looked, every chance he got. And that was often.

He was always willing to help around the house, no matter how many errands I asked him to run. He never complained. He told me that he had been well-trained at home, having run many errands for his parents over the years. That amazed me, and it was yet another quality I loved about him. I had heard many stories from other wives about how hard it was to get their husbands to do certain things, but that was never an issue with him. His willingness to help made me proud and appreciative.

He loved teaching me things, and he would get very excited when I asked questions that allowed him to share his knowledge. He did so with humility, never feeling the need to show off how brilliant he was. I was proud of his gifts, and I never failed to let others know. I always spoke well of him, bragging about him to my friends.

He loved to plan surprises, and I was often the beneficiary of his thoughtful gestures. I would receive surprise notes, and he always found ways to make me feel special. I saw how much he loved my family, especially my mother and son. When my mom needed something done, she would call him first because she knew he would be willing to help. He was a man with great family values, and that was one of the qualities I loved most about him. He was kind and extremely generous, always willing to help as much as possible, even if it meant making sacrifices.

Can someone do all of this without genuinely loving the person they're doing it for? I don't know. That question remains unanswered. But I was sure of one thing: he loved God with all his heart. As a Christian, I know that we can love God and still displease Him with our actions. I've done it myself many times. But I'm so grateful that God is forgiving, that none of us is too far gone for Him to restore when we come to Him with humility.

The Bible says, "If my people, who are called by my name, will humble themselves and pray and seek my face and turn from their wicked ways, then I will hear from heaven, and I will forgive their sin and heal their land." (2 Chronicles 7:14 NIV)

There were days when I felt my husband's love deeply, and there were days when I didn't. At times, he was hard to read and hard to understand. He didn't often express his feelings verbally, and when he did, it was usually after a buildup of emotion. When that happened, it wasn't so much a conversation as it was an attempt to make a point. We didn't listen to each other's hearts; instead, we were more focused on defending our positions.

There were many times when I would see a pondering look on his face, a look of deep contemplation and seriousness. I knew what love was supposed to look like; I'd been in love before, and I knew what it felt like to be loved. But with him, it was different. There were moments when I felt like we were going through what might be called a "silent divorce," where we were no longer sharing our true feelings about the critical matters surrounding us.

And yet, despite everything, I felt a strange sense of safety with him that I couldn't quite explain. It was as if he was saying, "I'm here, no matter what." Was it because he had nowhere else to go? Was it because he was determined to stick it out with me, no matter the cost? He was an independent, working man who had lived alone before we were married. He had the choice and the ability to leave, but he didn't.

Did He Need the Support to Overcome?

My husband never accepted his struggle as natural behavior. I truly believe that he wanted to change. But I often wondered if fear played a role in his decision to get married. Did he think that his actions might destroy his life if he remained single? Did he lack the internal discipline to overcome the struggle on his own, and did he believe that marriage would provide the distraction and accountability he needed?

Though he didn't reveal his struggle to me before we got married, I know that having a wife would have demanded a certain level of restraint on his part. I may not have known the triggers, and I'm not sure if he understood them fully either. But I could recognize when his behavior would change, and in those moments, I would give him space to work through his emotions, hoping that he'd come around.

Perhaps having a family was a reason for him to make better decisions, knowing the consequences that could follow if he didn't. He had responsibilities now; he had to be home by a certain time, we had to plan things together, and it wasn't just about him anymore. He was part of a larger unit—a family. Marriage might have given him a new perspective and caused a paradigm shift in his mind.

But was he at a point where he felt paralyzed and defeated, thinking that change would never come? Did he love himself enough to do whatever was necessary to change, no matter how difficult it might be? Did he ever visualize what change could look like, what it would do for his life and our marriage? That might have been a powerful motivation.

His struggle didn't align with his values and goals. It would have prevented him from achieving those goals, so perhaps that was another motivation to change. I'm not minimizing his challenges, especially since the struggle had been part of his life for so many years, but I believed that change was possible for him.

The Bible says in Colossians 3:5-10, *"Put to death, therefore, whatever belongs to your earthly nature: sexual immorality, impurity, lust, evil desires, and greed, which is idolatry. Because of these, the wrath of God is coming. You used to walk in these ways, in the life you once lived. But now you must also rid yourselves of all such things as these:*

anger, rage, malice, slander, and filthy language from your lips. Do not lie to each other, since you have taken off your old self with its practices and have put on the new self, which is being renewed in knowledge in the image of its Creator."

As believers, we stood on the Word of God. We believed that if God said it, it was done. It wasn't up for discussion or dispute. We had many conversations about our beliefs, and this was something we were in total agreement on.

Was It Fear of Being Alone or Lonely?

There are many instances where a married person stays in an unhealthy relationship because they believe it's better to remain in it than to be alone. Our marriage wasn't perfect, but there were good things about it. And yet, we certainly had enough reasons to go our separate ways if we had chosen to do so.

The fear of being alone can negatively affect relationships, leading to feelings of insecurity that manifest in ways that cause tension and conflict. I don't know what loneliness felt like for my husband, as that's something personal and subjective, depending on the person's needs.

But I do know that living with a secret like his must have created feelings of isolation, making him believe that something was fundamentally wrong with him.

I imagined that this consumed his mind, keeping him in deep thought. I also imagined that it brought feelings of anxiety when he was around others. Though he believed in the Word of God, the question of identity may have been something he struggled with deeply.

I remember him moving quietly and cautiously, as if he couldn't trust anyone. Before we started dating, I wasn't sure what to think of him. He was very much into himself, and it seemed like there was a wall between him and those around him. He didn't socialize much, and when he was at events, he always seemed to be the first to leave, usually alone.

At social gatherings, he would often disappear for periods, leaving me to sit at the table while he was on the phone. It was apparent that he had difficulty forming new connections, or maybe it was his choice not to do so because he was self-conscious and not ready.

If you're suffering from loneliness or feeling alone, the Word of God says, *"The Lord is close to the brokenhearted and saves those who are crushed in spirit"* (Psalms 34:18 NIV). *"Turn to me and be gracious to me, for I am lonely and afflicted. Relieve the troubles of my heart and free me from my anguish"* (Psalms 25:16-17 NIV). *"He heals the brokenhearted and binds up their wounds"* (Psalms 147:3 NIV).

Was He in Denial?:

I remember a conversation between my husband and me where I asked him a question about the same-sex lifestyle. He was very stern in his response, making it clear that he had never been in an ongoing sexual relationship with anyone. He didn't want to be labeled or associated with that lifestyle.

But was he in denial? Was he denying the reality of the situation, especially knowing that he was now married and the potential consequences that could follow?

Now, I'm no expert in psychology or psychiatry, so I can't claim to fully understand the thoughts and emotions of someone with an attraction to the same sex. However, because such a lifestyle would challenge deeply held beliefs, I believe it would be easy to fall into denial. It's a way to avoid facing complex problems, especially when one lacks the emotional capability to accept what's happening.

In our marriage, I had to deal with him justifying and minimizing serious issues, which was unhealthy for both of us. There was avoidance when I tried to talk about specific issues and defensiveness when I brought up important topics.

Talking about it would bring up emotions he wasn't willing to deal with, often leaving me feeling hopeless. I carried emotional confusion and, at times, silent rage. I may have been in denial myself, ignoring the signs that were probably there before we got married.

There was always the question of whether he could even be attracted to me, a straight woman. And the truth is, regardless of whether or not he felt lonely, I was a lonely wife. We lived together, but the atmosphere didn't add up or make sense to me. I wanted the intimacy that is expected in a marriage—the feeling of being wanted.

I spent a lot of time thinking about what I could do to change the situation, to keep him interested in me. I had a healthy sex drive, after all; that's one of the reasons I got married, based on my Christian beliefs. But it felt like hard work. There was too much tension and too much uncertainty.

Sometimes, I think that if fornication weren't a sin, many Christians would choose to remain single, living with their partners instead of marrying them. Marriage comes with expectations, responsibilities, and challenges that aren't always easy to meet.

No one knew what I was dealing with for the first seventeen months of our marriage. So, you can imagine the strain of having to put on a facade, pretending that everything was fine. I can compete with another woman, but how do you compete with a man? It felt impossible; I didn't have the same tools or appeal.

At that time, it didn't even occur to me to do any research that might have given me some insight and understanding. I was too caught up in my own confusion, too wrapped up in my own pain.

Before meeting my husband, very early in my Christian journey, I remember praying and asking God a question about someone. He spoke to me and led me to what is still one of my favorite Bible verses today: "Trust in the Lord with all your heart and lean not on your own understanding; in all your ways submit to him, and he will make your paths straight" (Proverbs 3:5-6 NIV).

This scripture has stayed with me throughout my life, especially in my marriage. During that time, I learned that no matter the circumstances I faced, God was in it. I made it a habit to commit everything to Him. God was my friend, my confidant, the one who would never leave me.

CHAPTER 6:

His Return - Reuniting:

Imagine this: after twenty-seven long months apart, with no meaningful, deep conversation about what had happened, we were now about to reunite and live together again. That was the situation I found myself in— a situation I chose to be in. How do you move forward from something like this? Could we rebuild our marriage and have a successful future together after everything that had transpired? During the time he was away, he worked doing what he loved best: teaching. He also attended the church he was familiar with and spent much time praying and focusing on himself and how to gain the victory he wanted over his struggle.

I decided to meet my husband where he was staying so we could travel home together. I remember watching him say goodbyes, telling the people he was leaving behind how much he would miss them. But what struck me and disappointed me deeply was that there was no expression of excitement about reuniting with me—no indication that he was looking forward to being with his wife again. It was as if I was just another stop on his journey.

I felt hurt, and I couldn't help but think that he needed to show both me and his friends that he wanted this marriage, that he wanted me. When I brought this up to him months later, it seemed like he hadn't even realized what he had done. I tried to understand that maybe he was nervous about returning home, unsure of what to expect, but that didn't make it any easier to accept. I had never stopped supporting him while he was away, so he knew I was still in this with him. I was willing to work on our marriage, to give it another shot.

I remember that hot day in July when we came home together as if it were yesterday. It felt like a new beginning, a fresh start. I was hopeful and filled with great expectations. I looked forward to a new season in our marriage—one that I hoped would be marked by love, connection, and, yes, passionate sex. Though I had visited him occasionally, reuniting in our home felt different, exciting, and full of promise.

As I reflect on that time, I can see how God orchestrated every step, keeping me in my right mind. He is the master storyteller, the architect of my life, and I am grateful for how He guided me through those difficult moments. But now, I found myself in a place where I had to resist fear and doubt. There was a war against my faith, and it seemed like God was taking too long to fix things. But I couldn't doubt His faithfulness. His timing is not ours, and I had to keep reminding myself to trust Him. I had hope and the assurance that something good would come of this. With God, all things are possible. I had to remember all the times He had brought me through challenging situations in the past, and I knew He would do it again. I had to see His Glory and His excellence because I believed He had great things in store for us. My stance was to fight the good fight of faith.

A Second Chance:

During the time we were apart, neither of us seriously considered dissolving our marriage. I didn't expect him to be away for so long, but that's how it happened. The delay was on him, and eventually, the decision had to be made: did he want to keep this marriage or not? The first few days after his return were tense, both for me and, I imagine, for him as well.

I knew he was in his head, wondering if I still wanted him sexually, if I had truly forgiven him, or if I saw him as a man who had failed his wife. What would our family and friends think now? And what about the church? Yes, we had sexual intercourse after his return, but it was clear that our problem wasn't going to magically disappear. There was much work to be done, and I thought this was the time to start. But even though we were united again with our community, it felt like we were left to figure things out on our own. Sure, there was general encouragement from various sources, but what we really needed was deep, meaningful help.

We knew how to pray up a storm, but we didn't pray together nearly as much as we should have. We didn't speak into each other's lives frequently enough. I knew we needed therapy, but I don't think either of us was ready to open up about such intimate issues to anyone else. There was still too much pride and shame in the mix. My husband spoke privately to our leaders, but I wasn't privy to what he shared with them. Once again, I was left out of the meaningful discussions that could have given me insight and understanding into his struggle.

I felt like I was in the lion's den, but no one would have known that by looking at me. I was thrilled to have my husband home, but it wasn't easy—it was far from it. It didn't take long before we were back to square one, with little sexual activity between us. It was as if nothing had changed.

Getting anything out of my husband that would help me understand was like pulling teeth. Whenever I asked a question, it was never the right time, or I was told that I was disturbing his spirit and that he didn't want to take his mind there. He refused to delve deep into any question I had. Any conversation about sex made him visibly uncomfortable, with a painful look on his face. Even when I tried to lighten the mood with sex jokes, he didn't laugh the way the average man would. That didn't exactly make me feel excited about approaching him sexually.

One day, we were driving, and he said to me, "I'm not the average man that when I see you naked, I want to have sex right away." In my mind, I thought, tell me something I didn't already know. Another time, we went shopping, and he saw a piece of lingerie that he liked. I secretly bought it, thinking that if he liked it, it might help spark something. Later that night, I showered, put on the lingerie, and walked into the living room where he was sitting. I did my best Victoria's Secret model impression, hoping to catch his attention. But his response was, "It would take more than that."

I was so hurt that I went to bed and cried. How could this be the same husband I had fully supported, the man I had stood by through everything? When I asked about his past, it was as if I had touched on a secret he couldn't share with me. Was he only covering for himself, or was he protecting someone else as well? We continued down this same path for a long time, with me walking on eggshells around him, sacrificing my happiness and peace of mind.

Though we did fun things outside the home with friends and family, I carried an ongoing sadness inside me. Most discussions or criticisms turned into arguments, and he would deflect by bringing up something about me that he didn't like. It was a tactic to distract from the original concern I had raised, and it led to no solutions. If I wasn't strong enough to stand my ground, it would have been easy to take the blame for his behavior. Whenever I disagreed with his point of view, I was accused of not understanding him, and he would later use that as an excuse not to share things with me.

But how could I understand him if he chose not to give me the information I needed? It was obvious that there was much he wasn't saying. I often told him that just because I disagreed with him didn't mean I didn't understand him. I was allowed to have a different opinion, but that seemed to trigger him too. I'm sure it stemmed from his past, which he still wouldn't let me into.

I went along with this for years until it became too much. I was tired of crying myself to sleep while my husband stayed awake, doing whatever he did. There was one night when I was so hurt that I cried in bed, and he showed no compassion whatsoever. I tried talking to him, but there was no response. He was cold and distant. I left the bedroom and called our leader and his wife, who had to console me over the phone. I wanted to leave the house, but it was too late to go anywhere.

That night was one of the most vulnerable I've ever experienced. I know that if there had been a man available whom I wanted to be with, I would have given myself to him that night. For the two years my husband was away, I'm proud that God kept me sexually pure. One would think that this was the perfect time for me to have an affair, but I didn't—not even once. Strangely, I had no interest in seeking anyone out during that time.

Men were there if I wanted them, but the desire wasn't. I kept telling myself that I didn't want any man to look at my husband and say, "I slept with your wife." That was very important to me. I didn't want to give my husband another reason to feel bad about himself.

We spent years repeating the same things over and over again. Going through the motions became a regular part of my life, smiling on the outside while carrying so much pain on the inside. I believe a few people around me were sensitive enough to see that something was wrong, but no one was bold enough to ask.

The Return to Our Community:

When my husband returned home permanently, many people were unaware of the timing. The leaders knew he would be at church that Sunday, but the general congregation didn't. I was nervous, and I'm sure he was too. We entered the building, and the stares started immediately. I could see the surprise on some faces, the wondering minds trying to piece together what had happened.

One of the things I heard from some folks during the time he was away was that I was stupid to stay with him. You know how it is—when you're not in the situation, you always know what you would do if it were you. There was a lot of that going around. But I was proud of my husband, and I was ready to continue supporting him for everyone to see. Many greeted him with hugs and smiles, expressing how happy they were to see him. Some were genuine, and some were not. I knew we were the topic of conversation at many lunch and dinner tables that Sunday.

He sat quietly and cautiously, not showing much emotion. He had left the comfort zone where he had been staying, where he had friends, and now he was back to his real life. Our leader arranged for a few members to gather at his home one evening, inviting us as well, to welcome my husband back and help him integrate into the community again. That was thoughtful, but as you can imagine, it wasn't an easy transition.

My husband was uneasy about building male friendships because he didn't want them to think he had ulterior motives, so he refrained from reaching out. I imagine that created feelings of loneliness for him. On the other hand, I had friends and was very sociable. He wasn't invited to many private men's gatherings because he didn't try to be friendly.

I remember one Sunday when someone was making announcements and acknowledged my husband's presence. But then he added, "He looks very gay." It was his way of trying to say he looked happy, but it wasn't funny at all; it was insensitive and hurtful. I'm not sure if my husband heard it, but I sure did, and I brought it to his attention later. I felt it was important for him to know, especially since this was someone he would be interacting with regularly. We must be careful about what we say about others in their fallen moments; we never know what life has in store for us.

One of the things that must have been extremely difficult for my husband was the jokes that were repeatedly made from the pulpit about people struggling with his issue, long before he ever revealed it to anyone. These jokes continued while he sat there, keeping his secret for years. Even while he was away, the jokes didn't stop. And now, I had to sit and listen as others laughed, knowing that I was the wife of someone dealing with this struggle. Some people didn't like my confidence and didn't appreciate how I carried myself, so they were happy to have something to laugh about, thinking they were hurting me. But I never gave them the satisfaction of showing any hate or anger.

The situation was incredibly insensitive, both for him and for me. On many Sundays, I left church feeling like I didn't want to return, but I didn't waver in my faith. I believe the church must teach and uphold what the Bible says about all forms of sexual misconduct. However, it felt like same-sex misconduct received more attention and more laughs than any other. It was as if adultery and fornication were more acceptable when they involved the opposite sex.

I'm not excusing my husband, but I later understood why

he might have hesitated to talk to someone. After his return, the jokes didn't stop. I'm not saying the jokes were made deliberately toward him—he wasn't the only one with this struggle—but I believe there was a better way to address the issue. I've listened to many messages from other ministries teaching against sexual misconduct, but none of them had the congregation laughing about it Sunday after Sunday.

As the years went by, the leaders showed more sensitivity in how they presented the message, and a general public apology was made to the church as enlightenment came to the leaders about what the Word of God says. My husband and I appreciated that.

My husband noticed that anything with his name on it before he left was redone, and his name was removed. There was an effort to disassociate him as much as possible from the church; after all, the church had to be protected. Some people unfriended him on social media and never reached out to ask how he was doing when he needed them the most.

Upon his return, I often heard him say that he knew he was tolerated because of me. He had met me in the church, and I was described as a model Christian— someone who was faithful and loved by many. For him to come into the church, marry me, and then put me through this made a lot of people angry on my behalf. I understood their feelings; I might have felt the same way if he had done this to someone I cared about. The feeling of being tolerated made it uncomfortable for him to settle in again.

There were times when my husband might have been in his head about certain things due to his insecurities, but I knew that some of his feelings and observations were valid. At one point, my husband felt it was time to leave the church and spoke to our leader about it. I disagreed with him because I knew he wasn't hearing from God but was giving in to his discomfort. I told him I wasn't leaving. I've learned that there are times when we have to remain in the camp, even when we're hurting, to receive our healing.

After his conversation with our leader, I believe it opened his eyes and heart to certain things, and he decided to stay. He sat without serving for quite a while, then slowly got back into service for the Kingdom since that was one of his passions.

I Had Enough:

One day, after a tearful conversation with my husband, I decided it was time for him to leave. We were ten years into our marriage at this point. Yes, I had dealt with this for that long. I was tired of carrying his emotions while neglecting my own. I was tired of always being the first to talk about what was happening in our marriage. He saw it, but he didn't show enough concern to initiate a conversation.

Whenever I wanted to speak, everything became about him, and I didn't feel like he was ready to accept full responsibility for what was happening to me. That would mean admitting that he was at fault. I had carried dead weight for years—both mine and his—and it felt like there was no end in sight. I was draining everything inside of me, and I didn't feel the need to be strong all the time anymore. We still hadn't learned how to communicate effectively with each other; it was more about proving our points without really listening.

I had exercised so much patience through the years, but I felt it was taken for granted. It was time to regain my joy, peace, and emotional health. I needed mental rest. I had given up so much of myself that my husband didn't know the real me. I struggled with not being wanted by my husband, the man I loved deeply and wanted very much. Like any other woman in a marriage, I needed love, not neglect. I carried confidence and knew I was wanted by other men, but that did not mean much to me; I wanted my husband to want me. It was hard for both of us mentally. At that time, I did not understand what he was dealing with and did not want to live like this anymore.

I was serious about him leaving. I didn't want him to think I was a pushover. Though I was ready to take that step, there was ongoing discomfort in my spirit. But I stuck to my decision and started helping him look for an apartment daily. I would ask him if he was actively searching for a place to live. I sent him links to apartments I thought would be suitable. I was even willing to help him financially to get started.

He didn't argue with me, and he didn't fight to keep the marriage. He felt I had good reasons to ask him to leave, so why should he fight to stay? That was a problem for me. Some might say it was about time, and I understand that perspective. I had finally reached the point where I told myself that I deserved to be loved the way I wanted.

He would tell me that he was looking for an apartment, but I didn't get the feeling that he was doing it with any urgency. I told one family member what was happening, and while she was supportive, she didn't think I should help him financially. But I wanted him to know I was serious, and I was willing to do whatever it took for him to get the message.

The foundation of our marriage was built on a lie, and at that time, it didn't seem like my efforts were making a difference. We needed to check into intensive care and stay there for a while. After all the praying and fasting, it seemed like nothing was changing. I got tired of hearing him say, "Don't worry, everything will be all right." That was his go-to response every time we had a conversation about our marriage, particularly our sex life.

How could it be all right if his behavior toward me wasn't changing? It was almost insulting, because I felt like he was just trying to appease me, putting a bandage on a wound that needed surgery. When you ask God to do whatever He wants in you, to make and mold you, be careful what you ask for. The fire was turned up in my life, and all this time, God was in the fire with me, preparing me for something greater. I was walking through a valley in the dark, but my valley walker was with me every step of the way.

"Even though I walk through the darkest valley, I will fear no evil, for you are with me; your rod and your staff, they comfort me." (Psalms 23:4 NIV) I had to remember that God is still God and that He is sovereign.

The Internal Struggle:

For the first time, I started seriously thinking about what life would be like without him—permanently. I loved him, and I wanted our marriage to work. I firmly believed that God had joined us together for a purpose. At the same time, I knew I had a choice about whether to continue the marriage, and I had valid reasons to end it.

Apart from the companionship of having a man in the house and someone to do fun things with, I started thinking about how helpful he was around the house and how much I would miss that if he were gone. I would now have to pay someone to fix things. I knew traveling would never be the same without him. Who would give me history lessons about the places we visited?

To some, these things might seem trivial, but they were meaningful to me. These were some of the things I loved about being with him. I told myself that if I ever got divorced from him, I would stay single for the rest of my life. I meant it, just as I did when I told God I was willing to remain single before I met my husband if that's what He wanted for me. I also knew that I could choose who I wanted because of who I was and what I brought to the table, but that was the furthest thing from my mind.

I wanted to believe that my husband wanted to try harder and do the right thing but didn't know how. Or maybe he wasn't ready to let go and get the healing he needed. Or perhaps he was just selfish in his ways and didn't care enough about me or our marriage. I thought about how he never once asked me if I had been unfaithful to him at any time. Was he afraid of the answer? Did he tell himself that I had the right to be unfaithful and would be okay with it if I didn't leave him? Or did he even care? I felt like I was his security plan.

He was deeply scarred and scared, but unless he was ready to get the help he needed, there was nothing I could do about it. During this time, he told me that he would sit alone and cry during his lunch breaks. It was touching to know that the idea of losing me made him cry. But where do we go from here?

If you've ever had to consider getting a divorce from a good man, you know my dilemma. The internal turmoil continued, and the questions kept coming. Was my marriage beyond repair after ten years of what often felt like a loveless partnership? Did I have any fight left in me? Could I take any more neglect and damage after being depleted of what I needed to cultivate a healthy relationship? Was he willing to do the work now? Were we at the point where neither of us could be bothered anymore?

I did my best to love him through it all, trying to see him through God's eyes, as my dear friend had advised me to. My husband met me during the best years of my life. Yet, I had given up so much of myself that he didn't know the real me. I had subdued some of the things I enjoyed because he wasn't interested. Now, I was questioning everything I thought I knew about love from a Christian man.

In this season of my life, I learned that it was necessary to set boundaries. By that, I mean that we teach people how to treat us. I had allowed too much for too long and should have been more assertive sooner. I should have been clear about what I would and wouldn't tolerate. My inner strength was slowly, inexorably eroding, and it had to stop. I needed a lot of wisdom and guidance to navigate this situation, and I couldn't afford to mess it up. I needed to know that I was making the right decision.

The following Bible verse became my anthem:

"If any of you lack wisdom, you should ask God, who gives generously to all without finding fault, and it will be given to you." (James 1:5 NIV)

CHAPTER 7:

Am I the Only One?

In the years since my experience, I've often wondered if I'm the only one who has gone through such a painful and complex journey. After all, I haven't encountered many books, journals, or open discussions about the secretive struggles surrounding same-sex attraction within heterosexual marriages, especially in

Christian communities. It's almost as if the topic is taboo, locked away in the deepest corners of our social consciousness. The lack of available resources or support groups for those dealing with these issues can lead to feelings of isolation and hopelessness.

In this chapter, I want to share what I've learned through research, personal reflection, and conversations with others who have faced similar struggles. Although it was challenging to find information on this topic, what I did uncover provided a sense of validation. It showed me that I am not alone, and perhaps this realization might bring comfort to others who are quietly battling the same demons.

The Secrets We Keep:

According to a study published in the journal Sexuality & Culture titled "The Sexual Secrets Men and Women Hide from Their Partners" (July 2021), many married couples keep sexual secrets. In fact, more than one- third of participants (36%) admitted to hiding at least one sexual secret in their current or most recent romantic relationship. Even more striking, over half (55%) of those surveyed revealed that they had shared a sexual secret with a partner at some point in the past. This suggests that while secrets may be kept for a time, they often eventually come to light.

The types of secrets people keep tend to differ based on gender. Women, for example, are more likely to keep sexual secrets because they believe their partner wouldn't understand. Men, on the other hand, are more likely to hide such information because they fear their partner wouldn't approve of their behavior.

For women, the most common secrets they kept from their partners were:

❖ A history of sexual victimization.

❖ Emotional infidelity.

❖ Interest in BDSM.

❖ Pornography use.

❖ Enjoyment of sex toys.

The reasons for keeping these secrets are varied, but they often include fear of judgment, shame, or concern that revealing them would end the relationship. For many, the stakes are too high to risk honesty, leading them to carry these secrets in silence.

As a woman, I can relate to the weight of carrying sexual secrets. I remember being about ten years old when a family friend visited our home. While my family member was in another part of the house, this person entered my room and attempted to touch me inappropriately.

Even at that young age, I knew his intentions were far from innocent. Thankfully, there wasn't enough time for anything more to happen, but the memory of that encounter has stayed with me all these years. It's a secret I've carried, never sharing it until now.

On another occasion, while I was in the care of a family member, someone in that household tried to persuade me to have sex with him.

I was thirteen years old and terrified. Nothing happened again, but the fear and confusion left deep scars. I often wonder how these experiences have shaped my views on intimacy and trust.

The Hidden Lives of Married Men:

I found another study titled The Psychological Being of Heterosexually Married Men Who Have Sex with Men, conducted by Seng Poh Lee in 2016. This study delves into the sexual satisfaction and psychological well- being of men who, despite being in heterosexual marriages, engage in sexual activities with other men. Sexual satisfaction, as defined by the World Health Organization (2010), is an essential component of sexual health, a marker of well-being, and a basic human sexual right. However, it's a complex and nuanced concept, shaped by emotional, relational, physiological, social, and cultural factors.

One participant in the study was asked about the difference between having sex with men and women and what sex with a man meant to him. He responded by describing sex with a man as a "lustful sexual experience." He found it physically more stimulating and satisfying than sex with a woman, noting that the mutual understanding and arousal shared with another man made the experience more exciting. In contrast, he described sex with a woman as more loving and caring.

The narratives from these men revealed that same- sex experiences were often more thrilling and sexually arousing, partly due to the illicit nature of the act compared to the 'normalcy' of marital sex. The fear and anxiety of being caught added a heightened sense of excitement, making same-sex encounters more desirable. This phenomenon aligns with clinical experiences reported by Corley and Kort (2006), where some men seek to 'increase their sexual nirvana through intense and increased risk.'

While this situation is unique, I've spoken with heterosexual men who shared similar feelings about extramarital affairs with women. They described the thrill of the forbidden, the excitement of secrecy, and the heightened satisfaction from these encounters, despite the resulting guilt and shame.

Another section of the study, Ease and Appeal of Opportunities for Engaging in Same-Sex, highlights that these men often seek same-sex encounters in specific locations such as parks, public restrooms, and certain commercial establishments like saunas or bathhouses. These environments provide a highly charged erotic atmosphere where sexual gratification is often readily available.

My husband once confided in me that parks and spas were places where he could easily find other men if he wanted to. Hearing this from him and reading similar accounts in the study made me realize how widespread this issue is. It also reinforced that I was not alone, that my husband was not alone, and that this is an issue the church needs to address openly. Many people sit in churches every Sunday, serving faithfully with smiles on their faces but harboring deep sadness and secrets within their hearts. I know this because I was one of those people, and so was my husband.

The Addictive Nature of Same-Sex Desires

The study further discusses the addictive triggers for same-sex desires. The participants identified several needs that compelled them to seek out same-sex encounters.:

A desire to be the receiver A high sex drive Excess free time or boredom Easy access to the internet A need for space away from married life Struggles with the addictive nature of same-sex desires The addictive nature of these desires was the most challenging aspect for participants. I believe this was also true for my husband. It's easy for those who haven't faced such struggles to dismiss them, saying, 'They should just stop,' or labeling them as 'sick.' But as a

wife who lived with a man struggling with these desires, I can tell you it's not that simple.

I also know heterosexual men who are seriously addicted to sex with women. They, too, need help, even though their behavior is more socially acceptable. Their struggles can also destroy marriages, leaving behind a trail of broken relationships and shattered lives.

One participant in the study expressed his feelings of guilt and shame, admitting that he often told himself it would be the last time, only to find himself returning to the same behavior. The deceit, dishonesty, and constant lying weighed heavily on his conscience, leaving him morally conflicted. He knew what he was doing was wrong, but the addictive nature of his behavior made it difficult to stop.

The Female Perspective

Not all women experience same-sex desires early in life. For some, these desires and behaviors emerge much later, often after they've already married men and lived as heterosexuals. Some women marry men out of genuine heterosexual attraction, only to discover or acknowledge their same-sex desires later on.

The term fluid lesbian refers to a woman who has alternated between lesbian and non-lesbian identities over time (Diamond, 2005). A lesbian is a woman whose sexual and romantic attractions are primarily toward other women (Rosenthal, 2013).

According to Buxton (2004), in about 2 million marriages between a man and a woman, one of the spouses is bisexual, gay, or lesbian. When one partner discloses their sexual minority status, about one-third of these couples attempt to stay married, while the other two-thirds decide to end their relationships. Additionally, between a quarter and a third of women who now identify as lesbian were once married to men (Kitzinger & Wilkinson, 1995). This number is likely underreported because many women choose not to come out at all.

Understanding the transition and developmental processes of previously married lesbian women is crucial in helping them build positive self-identities. It's also important to consider their past and present experiences within a social context.

The Christian Perspective

Finding information on this topic from a Christian perspective was the most challenging, which only reinforces my belief that the church needs to step up and address these issues. There is a desperate need for open discussions and guided therapy for married couples dealing with same-sex attraction. Too many people are suffering in silence, feeling that they have no one to turn to for help.

First, let me clarify my beliefs as a Christian. I believe in the Father, the Son, and the Holy Spirit. I believe that

Jesus is the Son of God who came to earth, died for my sins, was resurrected, and will come again to judge humanity. I believe in the Holy Bible, and everything written in it, and I strive to live according to God's word, though I have failed many times. For me, there is only one true and living God.

Regarding homosexuality, I believe it is a sin, as outlined in biblical teachings. The scriptures do not affirm homosexual activity, same-sex marriage, or changes in sexual identity. Leviticus 18:22 states, 'Do not have sexual relations with a man as one does with a woman; that is detestable.' However, I also believe that those who struggle with homosexual behavior, like any other sin, can be reconciled to God. As believers, it's our responsibility to encourage and support one another in our struggles.

The Pain of Being in a Heterosexual Marriage:

When I look back at my own experience, I realize I was not alone, though it felt that way at the time. Many others have walked a similar path, grappling with the pain, confusion, and betrayal that comes with discovering a spouse's same-sex attraction. It's a lonely journey, one that many are hesitant to speak about openly.

According to the study Egodystonic Homosexuals in Heterosexual Marriages: A Study of Christian Discourse (Vol. 4, September 2023), marriage should be based on love, not coercion or an attempt to hide one's sexual orientation. Homosexuals must understand the responsibilities of marriage before God and their spouse. Premarital counseling is essential, as it helps individuals understand their orientation, the foundation of Christian marriage, and the potential challenges they may face.

Such counseling can also help couples make informed decisions about their future together. The hope is that through understanding and guided therapy, individuals and couples can navigate their struggles in a way that honors God and strengthens their relationship.

The Loneliness of the Christian Struggle:

In my research, I came across a study titled Religiosity Among LGBT Adults in the U.S. by Karen J. Conron and Ethel Oct (2020). The study reveals that about 5.3 million LGBT adults in the U.S. are religious, with an estimated 3 million identifying as moderately religious and

2.2 million as highly religious. Among these religious

LGBT adults, about one in seven is married to a same-sex partner, while one in five is married to a different-sex partner. Additionally, many are separated, divorced, or widowed.

This study highlights the significant number of religious LGBT individuals who navigate the complex intersection of faith and sexuality. It underscores the need for the church to provide support and guidance for those struggling with same-sex attraction while maintaining their commitment to their faith.

Compassion and Understanding:

After conducting research for this chapter, I've gained a deeper understanding of the struggles faced by those with same-sex attraction who genuinely desire change. I now have more empathy for their experiences, including the shame, guilt, and inner loneliness that often accompany these struggles.

Please understand that I am not condoning this behavior in any way. However, as Christians, we have a responsibility to speak against sin while also teaching about the redemptive love of God. We must extend the same love and compassion that God showed us when we were in our own struggles.

I cannot tell any couple what to do; that decision rests between them and God. Each of us has our own journey, and while we may share similar paths, our destinies are unique. My prayer is that you will seek God's guidance in your journey and make choices that align with His will for your life.

For those who believe there is nothing wrong with same-sex acts or same-sex marriages and who may question how a Christian can claim to love all people while rejecting certain behaviors, I say this: I respect your beliefs and do not seek to judge anyone. However, loving someone does not mean accepting behavior that goes against your beliefs. Just as you might love a child or spouse who makes choices you disagree with; God continues to love us even when we fall short.

I loved my husband throughout his struggle, and I felt a deep obligation to support him once he revealed his challenges to me. I was convinced that he did not view his same-sex attraction as acceptable behavior and that he genuinely wanted to change. To me, this reflects the essence of God's love—loving someone enough to help them through their struggles, even when it's difficult.

As I conclude this chapter, I hope my story and the insights I've shared will bring comfort to those who are silently struggling. You are not alone. Others have walked this path before you, and there is hope for healing and restoration. My prayer is that you find the strength and courage to face your challenges, knowing that God's love is always there to guide you through.

CHAPTER 8:

Forgive Him? How Can I?

Forgiveness is a word that rolls off the tongue so easily, yet it's a monumental task when put into practice—especially when the offense is deep and personal. Over the years, I've heard many people say, "I'll forgive, but I won't forget." On the surface, this sounds practical. After all, some memories never fade. But I believe that when people say they won't forget, it's not just about memory; it's often a reluctance to release the hurt, an unwillingness to let go of resentment. This phrase can imply that the offender's actions will be held against them, perhaps indefinitely. I know that feeling all too well because I've been there many times.

The challenge of forgiveness is universal, yet as Christians, it's one of the things we are most called to practice.

One day, I was listening to a sermon by Joyce Meyer. She asked the audience to raise their hands if there was someone they hadn't forgiven. I was taken aback when she mentioned that at least 70% of the audience had their hands raised. I thought, how astonishing that the very act defining Christ's sacrifice for us—His forgiveness of our sins—is the same thing that many Christians struggle with the most. Jesus bore our sins on the cross, offering us grace and forgiveness, yet we often find it difficult to extend the same to others.

Ephesians 4:32 (NIV) says, "Be kind and compassionate to one another, forgiving each other, just as in Christ God forgave you."

Colossians 3:13 (NIV) echoes, "Bear with each other and forgive one another if any of you has a grievance against someone. Forgive as the Lord forgave you."

Matthew 6:15 (NIV) warns, "But if you do not forgive others their sins, your Father will not forgive your sins."

Why Is It So Hard to Forgive?

Forgiveness is challenging because it cuts against the grain of our human nature. We're born into sin; disobedience to God is in our DNA from the moment we enter this world. Every one of us needs God's forgiveness, and He has graciously provided a way for all our sins—past, present, and future—to be forgiven. Yet, when it comes to forgiving others, we struggle. I found it hard to forgive in the past for two main reasons: first, the lingering pain kept the offense alive in my mind, and second, I often thought others' sins were worse than mine. I'm sure many can relate to this.

When we don't forgive, we give the offender power over our thoughts, actions, and feelings. Holding onto anger and resentment is like carrying a heavy burden that drains us emotionally and spiritually. Early in my Christian walk, my leader shared a powerful statement that has stayed with me: *"Do not allow anyone to make you stoop so low that you hold unforgiveness and hate in your heart toward them."* This perspective opened my eyes—it *helped me see that forgiveness isn't just about the other person; it's also about my own well-being.*

Forgiving others has profound benefits: it keeps us from living with a bitter heart, grants us peace of mind, and, most importantly, aligns us with God's will. Unforgiveness is a sin, and it's even been linked to physical ailments. In John 5:14 (NIV), after healing a man who had been lame, Jesus warned him, *"Stop sinning or something worse may happen to you."* Scholars suggest that Jesus implied sin could bring even more severe consequences than the physical affliction the man had just been healed from.

It's also important to understand that forgiving someone doesn't necessarily mean you're obligated to stay in a relationship with them. Sometimes, it's necessary to remove yourself from a harmful situation, especially if there's ongoing physical, emotional, or mental abuse. Marriage is hard work, but it only works when both people are willing to put in the effort, walk in obedience, and follow the principles God has set for us.

I Chose to Forgive

Learning about my husband's struggle was one of the most painful experiences of my life. The revelation felt like a heavy blow, shaking the very foundation of our relationship. Yet, I made the conscious decision to forgive him—not just for keeping this part of his life hidden, but also for not giving me the chance to choose how I wanted to proceed before marriage. Forgiveness wasn't easy, but I chose it because I loved him and because I knew, deep in my heart, that forgiveness was the only path to true healing.

The pain, the betrayal, and the flood of emotions that accompanied his confession were undeniable and overwhelming. There were moments when the weight of it all seemed unbearable, but I also understood something vital: holding onto unforgiveness would only serve to hurt me further. More than anything, I wanted to honor God, and I knew that unforgiveness would create a barrier between me and Him. To nurture my own spiritual health and emotional well-being, I had to let go of the bitterness.

Forgiveness, I've come to learn, isn't just for the person who wronged us—it's for us as well. It frees our hearts from the chains of bitterness and resentment that, if left unchecked, can consume us. Over the years, I've discovered that when I forgive, healing comes more quickly, and the peace that follows is undeniable. There's a profound freedom in knowing I carry no grudges, and I've witnessed God reward that obedience time and time again. He has prepared a table before me, even in the presence of my enemies, and has blessed me as I've chosen to walk in humility. But that humility is key. When God vindicates us, we must guard against pride or arrogance creeping in. Forgiveness isn't about elevating ourselves; it's about reflecting God's grace.

Before my husband left to seek help, I made it a point to tell him that I had forgiven him. I knew how important it was for him to hear those words. He was already carrying an enormous burden, and the last thing I wanted was for him to feel that his wife was holding unforgiveness over him. Continuing our marriage with intention and authenticity required that forgiveness be at the center of our efforts to move forward.

I'm not sure if he fully believed me when I said I had forgiven him so quickly. Perhaps he doubted it, given the magnitude of his actions and the hurt they caused. But I knew I had forgiven him. I couldn't support him through his journey if I hadn't released the anger and pain. True forgiveness requires empathy, compassion, and an open heart. I had to place myself in his shoes, imagining the weight he had carried for so long, even though the choices he made had caused me deep wounds.

It's important to acknowledge that some sins carry heavier consequences than others. But forgiveness isn't about weighing sins on a scale or determining what deserves mercy. God didn't assign us the job of judging the sins of others; He simply called us to forgive. Often, our inability to forgive stems from a lack of understanding about someone's life experiences. We fail to consider what may have shaped their actions—the traumas, fears, or pain that influenced their decisions. True forgiveness requires us to step outside of our own limited perspective and consider the situation from the other person's point of view.

I didn't know all the details of my husband's life, and honestly, I didn't need to. When it came to forgiveness, his past didn't need to be fully understood or justified. What mattered was my choice to extend the same grace to him that God had so freely given me. I had been forgiven for much, and it was my duty to offer that same grace to the man I had promised to love. Forgiveness wasn't just about healing our marriage—it was about honoring the redemptive power of grace in both of our lives.

Our Road to Restoration

You might wonder how our story ends—unless, of course, you've skipped ahead to the last chapter. As of this writing, my husband and I have celebrated eighteen years of marriage, and we're happy together. To God be the glory!

I don't know what the future holds, but I pray we will continue to grow together for many more years. Like any marriage, we still have to work at it daily to make it successful.

Why did I choose to stay with him? What happened to his struggle? Several factors kept us together. In the previous chapter, I mentioned that I had asked my husband to leave the house. One day, while sitting under the hairdryer at my hairdresser's, I was talking to God, asking Him to confirm whether He wanted me to end my marriage. Since asking my husband to leave, I had felt a growing discomfort. After walking with the Holy Spirit for many years, I knew His voice and His guidance in my life. As I prayed, seeking God's direction, our leader—

who was aware of our situation and had been praying for us—called me and said, "God wants you to stay in your marriage." I wasn't surprised, as it confirmed what I had already sensed in my spirit. I trusted our leader because I knew he was a man who heard from God and wouldn't treat such a serious matter lightly. Now, I had to obey and trust God. Instantly, the peace I had been waiting for filled me.

But it takes two to make a marriage work. My husband had to decide to fight for our marriage, confront his struggles, and choose to change. When we talked about what brought about his change, he said simply, "I made a decision." He explained that, regardless of how well someone understands their weaknesses or how much therapy they receive—though therapy certainly helps—they ultimately have to decide to change. Therapy became a significant part of his life, helping him confront and overcome his struggles.

You might wonder why it took so long for him to make that decision, and I don't have a definitive answer. However, I believe that God had a purpose in the timing. If change had come too quickly, I wouldn't have had the experiences necessary to write this book, and perhaps many who need to hear this story wouldn't have the opportunity to read it.

I knew when change finally came. The heaviness that had weighed on our marriage lifted, and the atmosphere in our home felt lighter. God had started something new in our marriage, and I could feel it. But the change wasn't just required from my husband; it was required from me as well.

I had to confront and change some destructive behaviors in my personal and spiritual life. I had to adjust my thinking, reevaluate certain relationships, and align my life more closely with God's will. Sometimes we pray for others to change, only to realize that God is asking us to change first.

Forgiving Myself

You might wonder what I needed to forgive myself for. Well, remember when I said we teach others how to treat us? I had to forgive myself for not standing up for myself when I should have, for remaining silent when I should have spoken out, for not seeking therapeutic help sooner, and for not insisting that my husband get the help he needed earlier. I had a responsibility to myself—as a human being, as a woman, as a mother, and as a wife. In my concern for everyone and everything around me, I neglected my own mental and emotional well-being.

Forgiving myself meant accepting the past for what it was and refusing to dwell on it. It was painful to take a deep dive into my past mistakes, but it was necessary to secure a positive, bright future. I learned what I needed to about myself, extended grace to myself, and showed myself the same compassion I had shown to others. The enemy wants to keep us bound to our past mistakes, filling us with guilt and unworthiness. But God isn't keeping track of our mistakes, and neither should we. Romans 8:1-

2 (NIV) reminds us, "Therefore, there is now no condemnation for those who are in Christ Jesus, because through Christ Jesus the law of the Spirit who gives life has set you free from the law of sin and death."

Forgiving the Church

I love my church and the people in it. I have joyfully and faithfully served there for a quarter of a century as of the writing of this book. But, like any family or social structure, the church is not immune to causing hurt. There are times when leaders, though well-meaning, don't always make the right decisions. Church hurt is a common experience, and I'm sure that, at some point, I've unintentionally hurt someone in the church as well.

Given the situation my husband and I were facing, I believe the leaders wanted what was best for us and the church at the time. I won't question the intent of anyone's heart because only God knows the truth. I can only speak from my experience and how certain decisions affected me. No one can truly understand what I felt during those challenging times unless they've walked in my shoes.

With that in mind, I realized I needed to forgive my church for several reasons. Throughout this situation, leaders frequently expressed how much they respected and admired me, which I genuinely appreciated. Outwardly, I remained strong and continued serving without missing a beat, but my inner struggles went unnoticed. Because I appeared strong, it was assumed I was coping well on the inside, and no one pursued the professional help I truly needed.

Looking back, I realize the church may not have had experience dealing with a situation like ours, so there was no established protocol for helping someone deeply affected by a spouse's struggles. Yes, I received calls and messages asking how I was doing, which I appreciated, but there was also a sense of homophobia among some, which prevented them from ministering to us as we needed. In retrospect, I recognize that some were dealing with their own issues, which may have hindered them from providing the support we required.

My hope is that if another marriage like ours faces similar hardships, my story will serve as a learning experience for the church leaders. It was important for me to demonstrate the love of God as I understand it, so I pressed through the pain and remained committed. I acknowledged the hurt, continued to pray, and built my faith, learning what to hold on to and what to let go of.

I chose to stay with my church community because I never believed God wanted me to leave, even though there were many Sundays when I didn't want to be there. God planted me in that church for a purpose, one greater than any situation or person. My goal has always been to please God because I knew the enemy wanted me to walk away from my calling. But I stood firm, and I won.

Forgiveness is a journey, not a one-time event. It's a process of letting go, healing, and moving forward. It's about choosing to release the pain and resentment, not just for others' sake but for our own. It's about trusting God to work in our hearts and in the hearts of those who have wronged us. It's about believing that with God, all things are possible, including the restoration of what was once broken.

CHAPTER 9:

Purpose in the Pain - Why I Stayed.

Many of you might be wondering: why did I stay? Why endure the pain, betrayal, and hardship? It's a fair question and one I've asked myself countless times. When I look back on this journey, I see parallels in the Bible with characters who suffered great hardships— abandonment, rejection, betrayal, loss—yet found profound purpose in their pain. There was always a greater plan, even when the enemy meant it for evil. God always showed up, transforming the pain into something greater, something purposeful. Their stories weren't just about them; they were meant to bless, encourage, and strengthen others. I believe that my story, too, would ultimately bring hope and healing to many.

Before I married my husband, I prayed long and hard. My decision wasn't driven by emotion or any overwhelming attraction. I wasn't *"wowed"* into marriage by him, even though I knew he was a good man. But deep in my heart, there was a love I couldn't explain, a peace I couldn't deny. I knew that this love wasn't something I created on my own—it was from God. I've often told my husband that God placed that love for him in my heart. On our wedding day, there was such peace, such a tangible presence of God in the sanctuary. Even today, friends who were there still talk about that experience.

When God gives you a vision or a path, you must learn to block out the noise—the well-meaning opinions, the doubts of others—because they don't know the plan He has for you. They can only see the outside; they cannot understand the intricate process God uses to prepare us for greatness.

I remember a conversation I had with my leader when I was frustrated and complaining about my husband. He offered a perspective I hadn't considered, saying, *"Don't be like Adam and Eve, who focused on what they didn't have, forgetting the good that was already theirs."* He reminded me that my husband was a good man, and I *needed to shift my focus. On another occasion, I spoke to him about feeling alone despite having many friends. He explained that every person God uses for great things must endure a wilderness season—a period of isolation and preparation. He was right.*

The Character of Job:

No one in the Bible seems to have suffered more than Job. He had everything: family, wealth, and a good name. Then, in what seemed like a cruel twist, God allowed Satan to take it all away. Job lost his children, his wealth, and even his relationships. Yet, through it all, he chose to praise God rather than curse Him. Job had moments when he questioned God and wrestled with his suffering, but he didn't stay there. He repented, humbled himself before God, and, in the end, God restored him. Job was rewarded with more than he had lost because he remained faithful.

Job's story reminds me that there is always purpose in our pain.

Job 1:20-21 (NIV*): "At this, Job got up and tore his robe and shaved his head. Then he fell to the ground in worship and said: 'Naked I came from my mother's womb, and naked I will depart. The Lord gave and the Lord has taken away; may the name of the Lord be praised.'"*

The Character of David:

David, the anointed king of Israel, was chosen by God, but his path wasn't easy. He endured years of torment from King Saul, who was jealous of him and sought to kill him. David was forced to hide, living in caves and relying on others for sustenance. Despite his hardships, David had the opportunity to kill Saul but chose not to. His heart remained good, even in the face of immense suffering. And through it all, David continually turned to God in praise.

David's story taught me that even when things seem unbearable, faith in God's plan will lead to victory.

Psalms 142:1-2 (NIV): "I cry aloud to the Lord; I lift up my voice to the Lord for mercy. I pour out before him my complaint; before him I tell my trouble."

The Character of Moses:

Moses' story is one of great suffering and responsibility. He was tasked with leading the Israelites out of Egypt, only to face endless challenges and complaints from his people. Even after parting the Red Sea, Moses was tested again and again. When the people lacked water, they grumbled, and Moses turned to God for help. God always provided. Moses learned to trust God in the wilderness, even when the path seemed impossible.

Moses' journey is a testament to perseverance and faith in the face of overwhelming odds.

Exodus 15:25 (NIV*): "Then Moses cried out to the Lord, and the Lord showed him a piece of wood. He threw it into the water, and the water became fit to drink."*

The Character of Peter:

Peter is one of the most relatable figures in the Bible because of his very human failures. He promised Jesus that he would never deny Him, yet when the time came, Peter denied Jesus three times. The weight of his failure broke him. Peter wept bitterly and thought he was unworthy of the calling on his life. But Jesus, in His love, restored Peter and gave him a second chance. Peter went on to live a life fully devoted to Christ, even dying by crucifixion for his faith.

Peter's story shows that failure isn't the end. God can restore anyone willing to return to Him with a repentant heart.

Mark 14:72 (NIV): "Immediately the rooster crowed the second time. Then Peter remembered the word Jesus had spoken to him: 'Before the rooster crows twice you will disown me three times.' And he broke down and wept."

John 21:16 (NIV): "Again Jesus said, 'Simon son of John, do you love me?' He answered, 'Yes, Lord, you know that I love you.' Jesus said, 'Take care of my sheep.'"

Through these characters, I learned that all things are possible with God. During the most challenging times, I found strength, guidance, and comfort in Him. Even when we don't understand what God is doing, He is always at work. Isaiah 55:9 (NIV) reminds us, "As the heavens are higher than the earth, so are my ways higher than your ways and my thoughts than your thoughts."

I clung to that truth, knowing God wasn't leading me into a dead-end. His plans for me were good, even when I couldn't see it. Faith and patience became my lifelines. So many people give up too soon, not realizing that the deeper the roots, the taller the tree. I could have left, and no one would have blamed me. But leaving wasn't what God wanted for me. His love would have covered me no matter what, but the real question was: Would I have fulfilled my purpose?

It took me seven weeks to write this book, which might seem fast, but in reality, it took eighteen years of marriage. Every day of those years—through all the pain and struggles—God was pruning, shaping, and preparing me for this. He was depositing in me what He wanted me to give to the world. Now, that fruit was ripe, and it was time for the harvest.

When I think about how quickly I matured in my Christian walk, it's clear that God was preparing me for what was to come. My spiritual leader often mentioned how fast I seemed to grow in the Lord. People were surprised when they learned how few years I had been walking with God—they always assumed it was longer.

After my husband revealed his struggle, some said God had been preparing me for that moment by maturing me quickly, and I believe that's true. A spiritually immature person would not have survived this ordeal in a healthy way.

No Regrets:

Looking back, I have no regrets. There are things I would have done differently in my younger years if I knew then what I know now. But knowing how God wanted to use me, I would still choose my husband all over again. I now realize that our purpose together was bigger than both of us. One of my favorite songs is *"Lord, I'm Available to You,"* and I used to sing it on my knees, not fully understanding what I was asking. But I meant it. When God chooses to use you, He equips you for the journey— often through pain.

My love for God has deepened because of this journey. He has shown me time and time again that even in the most difficult circumstances, He is faithful. His plans are always good, and He can turn any situation for His glory. Even when it seemed impossible, God made a way.

Philippians 4:6 (NIV): *"Do not be anxious about anything, but in every situation, by prayer and petition, with thanksgiving, present your requests to God."*

A Marriage Meant for Ministry:

From the very beginning, my husband and I believed that our marriage was destined for ministry, though we didn't fully understand how. Over time, God began to reveal His plan to us, step by step. One thing I've learned about God is that He rarely lays everything out at once. Instead, He calls us to take small, faithful steps, trusting

Him to guide us along the way. His ways are intentional and strategic, and He uses our pain to shape us into vessels for His purpose.

God doesn't waste pain. He expects us to take the trials, failures, and poor decisions we endure and use them for a greater good. What we go through is never just for us—it's meant to serve and bless others. This book is my act of faith and obedience to that calling. I couldn't have written it until I was truly ready to release everything into God's hands, trusting Him to work through me.

If God is tugging on your heart to step out in faith and do something He's placed in your spirit, don't wait—just do it. You may not see the full picture right now, but trust that He's already at work, orchestrating something far beyond what you can imagine.

My deepest prayer is that this book will bless and inspire many. If it saves even one marriage, all the effort and vulnerability will have been worth it. As I write these words, I can feel God's presence, and the message He's placed in my heart is this: I brought you through so you can walk alongside others.

There is purpose in the pain. Even when it feels overwhelming, trust that God is up to something far greater than you can comprehend. Surrender your pain to Him, and He will transform it into something beautiful.

CHAPTER 10:

How to Help Your Spouse

Have you ever watched your spouse, or children struggle through something difficult and wished you could take their pain away? That was my experience throughout my marriage—time and time again, I saw my husband struggling internally, and I would find myself asking, how can I help him? There are battles we all must face alone to grow, but having the right support system can make those battles more bearable, sometimes even lighter.

My husband had developed an avoidant attachment, which made it hard for him to ask for help or rely on others. There was a fear of being a burden or facing rejection, especially if past attempts at vulnerability had been met with negative responses. But I was determined to be there for him, in whatever way I could, as much as he would let me. I knew that if he asked for help, it could stir feelings of shame. So, I took it upon myself to support him in the ways I thought would help, even when he couldn't or wouldn't ask. I'll share some of the things I did, hoping they may inspire you in your own journey.

1. I Did Not Blame Myself for His Behavior:

One of the first truths I had to accept was that my husband's struggle was not my fault. He entered our marriage carrying his own internal battles, and while I became an unfortunate casualty of those struggles, I was not their cause. This understanding was vital for preserving my confidence and self-esteem. If I had allowed myself to internalize his actions—blaming myself or feeling responsible—I would have been paralyzed by my own emotional pain. That kind of self-blame would have made it impossible to offer him the support he needed. To truly help him, I had to remain strong, even in the face of deep hurt.

One of the ways my husband coped with his pain was through projection—a psychological defense mechanism famously described by Freud as attributing one's own feelings, thoughts, or shortcomings to someone else. Projection creates distance from guilt or shame, providing a temporary escape from inner conflict. When my husband acted out in ways that were hurtful, I reminded myself that his behavior wasn't about me. It was his way of grappling with his own turmoil.

Understanding this was not easy, but it was essential. By recognizing that his actions stemmed from his internal struggles rather than any failure on my part, I was able to approach the situation with empathy instead of reacting out of anger or hurt. This perspective allowed me to maintain my emotional stability and resist falling into destructive patterns. Instead of being consumed by his projections, I focused on staying grounded, offering him the support he needed while protecting my own sense of self.

2. I Prayed for Him

As a woman of faith, I knew that prayer was my lifeline—not just for me, but especially for my husband. Deep in my heart, I believed that nothing was too hard for God. I prayed for my husband's healing, for the wounds in his mind and emotions to be replaced with peace and joy. I prayed that God would touch the deepest parts of his soul, bringing him into spiritual maturity. I asked God to help him release shame, guilt, and pride, and to soften his heart so he could hear God's voice.

My prayers weren't just about asking God to change him; I also prayed for the wisdom to support him in the ways he truly needed. I asked God to show me how to love him through his struggle, to be patient, and to offer the kind of support that would make a difference. I prayed that he would begin to see himself the way God saw him—that he would come to believe he was worthy of love and healing.

3. I Always Spoke Well of Him:

One of the things I committed to was speaking well of my husband, both in his presence and absence. My friends would tell you that no matter what I was going through in my marriage, I always found something to brag about when it came to my husband. Even when I was in pain, I chose to highlight the positives. I knew that some of my friends grew tired of hearing me talk about him, but I didn't care—I wanted my words to build him up, not tear him down.

Men need affirmation, especially when they struggle with feelings of inadequacy. I wanted to create a safe space for my husband, a place where he knew he was loved and valued. I wanted him to know that, despite his struggles, I still saw him as a great man. I was intentional about complimenting him, whether it was for his appearance, his cooking, or his work ethic. I spoke over his life, even when I didn't yet see the things I hoped for.

4. I Showed Appreciation and Admiration:

I made a point to thank my husband for the things he did, no matter how small. I didn't want him to feel taken for granted, and I didn't want to come across as entitled. Yes, there were things I expected from him as my husband, but I also knew the importance of showing gratitude. I made it a habit to say, "You see why I need you?" whenever he helped me with something, even if it was a small task. Those words always brought a smile to his face.

There were times when my husband doubted his value in our marriage, so I made it my mission to remind him of all the reasons I appreciated him. I complimented him on his looks, his intelligence, his creativity, and his dedication. I knew that if I didn't speak life into him, the negative voices in his head might take over.

5. I Took His Struggle Seriously:

I longed for a quick change, but I knew my husband's struggle was real and deep. While I didn't always understand it, I validated his feelings. I didn't lash out or belittle him, even when I was hurting. Instead, I chose patience and love, recognizing that I was the closest person to him and the one who saw him through spiritual eyes.

I engaged in small, meaningful gestures to show him I was there. I'd run up and hug him, leave little notes, or act silly just to make him smile. He once told me that my touch was healing, so I made it a point to reach out physically, even when words weren't enough. These weren't always things I instinctively knew to do—they were things I had to work on over time, and some I'm still working on. But I could see the difference it made in him, and that motivated me to keep going.

6. I Provided Emotional and Spiritual Support:

Providing emotional support when you're running on empty is no easy task, but I knew my husband needed to hear that I loved him and was there for him, no matter what. I became his biggest cheerleader, constantly reminding him that he could overcome whatever challenges he faced. When he vented, I learned to listen to what he wasn't saying and gently probed deeper. Even when I was tempted to tell him to "get over it," I held my tongue.

I'd ask how he was doing, even when I knew he'd say he was fine, and I encouraged him to open up when he was ready. When he asked for something specific, I did my best to give it to him. He'd tell you that my constant encouragement and patience were two things that helped him through—and those are qualities I didn't even know I had in me.

7. I Learned to Listen for What He Needed:

While everything I did was important, the key was knowing what my husband needed most at any given time. If you're not sure, ask. Early in our marriage, he'd lay his head on my lap and ask me to rub it. At first, I found it a little annoying, but as time passed, I realized how much it meant to him. Now, whenever we sit together or I walk past him, I instinctively reach out to touch his head because I know it comforts him. It's such a small gesture, but it made a world of difference for him.

Building a strong, supportive relationship comes from learning to give your spouse what they need, rather than what you think they need.

This list is by no means exhaustive. There are many things you can do to help your spouse through their struggles. The key is knowing your spouse, learning to communicate effectively, and being willing to grow together. My husband and I were at different levels of emotional maturity, and I had to extend patience to meet him where he was. I had to be a Christian seven days a week, not just on Sunday.

I also learned that with purpose comes warfare. The enemy will use anything and anyone—family, friends, coworkers, and even church members—to disrupt God's plan for your life. But I held on to the prophetic words spoken over my marriage and reminded God of His promises. I prayed for strength and discernment, knowing the enemy wanted to see our marriage fail, but I refused to give him that satisfaction.

If you are going through a difficult time in your marriage, especially if you have children at home, remember that they, too, need your love and attention. My son was a teenager when I married my husband, and I had to balance being present for both. I couldn't neglect my son or let him feel he was at fault for what I was going through.

Through it all, God reminded me to be still and know that He is God (Psalm 46:10 NIV). He instructed me to put on the full armor of God so that I could stand against the devil's schemes (Ephesians 6:11 NIV). The Word of God became my lifeline, and I am grateful for the exceptional teaching I've received on my spiritual journey. My leader's teachings on faith, patience, and resilience echoed in my mind as I navigated the hardest moments in my marriage.

Let me share one more story to show how God continues to confirm His will in my life. Two days after I finished writing Chapter 10, I went to church, as I always do. A visiting couple from Canada was there, and I didn't know them. The wife, an author, sat in the same row as me. Without any introduction, she walked over and handed me a book, saying she felt led to bless me with it. The title alone ministered to me before I even read the first page. She later signed it with the words, "Nothing you go through in life is ever wasted."

At the end of the service, I thanked her and mentioned that I was writing a book of my own. She looked at me and said, "God wants you to go forth." That was the confirmation I didn't even know I needed. It was God's way of telling me I was on the right path.

When I got home, I read the entire book in one sitting, and I was amazed to see that she and I had used many of the same scriptures and phrases in our writing. It was as if God had orchestrated our meeting to remind me that I'm not alone in this journey, that there is purpose in the pain, and that He is using it for His glory.

So, as you read this, know that God is with you, too.

He is guiding your steps, even when the way forward seems uncertain. Trust that He's working through you and your marriage—remember: God brought me through so I can be here with you.

My Husband Speaks for The First Time

"A Window into My Journey"

At the time of writing this, I have not read the preceding chapters of this book written by my wife. But here's a peek into our journey together.

It was a Friday morning, and as everyone found out about my double life, the very air around me seemed to reject my lungs, and my chest felt heavy and burdened. An overwhelming sadness kept building up inside. I called my closest friend at the time, a brother in church, and thankfully, he dropped everything to find me. I was literally walking down the street, crying almost uncontrollably. I felt lonely, abandoned, and completely destroyed.

Calling it self-sabotage doesn't quite capture it. I had never been in this place before. Fifty million thoughts and emotions consumed my mind all at once. What would people say and think of me? How would my family react? These were just a few of the many thoughts racing through my head. When my friend finally arrived, we drove to a local pier. For the first time, I took somebody on a walk down that road of my life and shared my journey. I told him, "I cannot feel God's presence." His response to me was, "It's not that God has abandoned you; you feel this way now because He's actually carrying you in His arms." The moment he said those words, deep wounds of despair began to heal for the first time.

In that complex, painful moment, I never once felt him judge me. He said, "Brother, I see you no differently than before." If I had $10 million right then, I would have given it to him. The restoration, personal value, and dignity that began rushing through me at his words were priceless.

Despite this, the time eventually came when this same friend cut off all communication, suddenly and without warning. So many years have passed, and of all the wounds in my heart, this one hurts the most. I don't hate him. To give him the benefit of the doubt, I've always assumed that people judge you by the company you keep. Perhaps I was no longer good enough to be called his friend or to be associated with him, given the path of his own life juxtaposed against any public perception of mine.

Realistically, I have to be okay with that. But it hurts like hell every time I think about it. With time, it has gotten better. After our conversation, he dropped me off at some close friends' house. That same day, my wife found out and left work early to come meet us. I felt as if the entire planet had fallen out from beneath my feet. On the way home in the taxi, I reached over to touch her right hand, and she pulled it away from me.

That night, as we lay in bed, I shared the story of my life's journey that I had tried so hard to run away from. She asked many questions—who, why, when, where, and how. She cried, and I cried. I felt terrible. She never raised her voice, cursed, or threatened me. I didn't want to hurt this beautiful woman whom I genuinely believed God had given to me as a gift. But before I met her, I was lonely and had fallen in love with a beautiful woman who became a kind and gracious friend. To this day, she is the only other woman I have ever been with.

When I was searching for a wife, I asked God to send me a woman with a list of qualities I had written down in prayer. Among many things, I asked for a woman who was a worshiper and loved the presence of God. At the top of the list, I asked God for a wife who would have the capacity to love me, despite the burdens I carried as a young man. In my heart, I wished she would never find out. But on a deeper level, I knew one day I would have to have a conversation that could potentially become a defining moment in our marriage.

Looking into the future, I knew that whatever shape my

private struggles with same-sex attraction might take, our spiritual maturity and commitment to each other would be tested. Despite the heavy knots I felt in my stomach and the sense that our marriage was hanging in the balance, I didn't feel hate coming from her. She was disappointed in me, hurt by how I had dishonored our marriage and broken her trust. Yet, despite it all, how she treated me in those moments began to heal my heart and mind in real time. She was the genesis of the second wave of restorative energy I felt that day, even if she still couldn't bring herself to hug me.

The next day, Saturday, I went to my office at our church to gather my personal effects. I'd been asked not to return until things were resolved. Despite the awkwardness, I was treated with respect. My colleagues waited for me to join them, but I simply greeted them from a distance and kept walking. I didn't know when I would see them again, and they had no idea I was leaving indefinitely.

Suddenly, my phone rang—it was my mother. She informed me that she would be arriving the following day, Sunday. When I picked her up from the airport, her face showed sadness, mixed with patience. Calmly, she expressed her disappointment in my choices and how she felt I had let down many people who had admired and respected me. Before she even landed, the consensus among my family was that I needed a change of environment; being in New York was just too much to handle.

That night, we stayed at my mother-in-law's house. It felt good to be loved by my family and to feel the genuine care they had for me, despite all they now knew. Still, there was a heaviness in the air—a sense of 'how- will-the-world-react' uncertainty. The following morning, in the dark hours before sunrise, I would be taking a one- way flight back to my home country.

Surprisingly though my wife and I had the best 'goodbye-makeup-I'm sorry-sex' ever. She still desired me!

In the early hours of the morning, the entire house was awake again. We gathered by the back door as I took my luggage out and began saying our goodbyes. My mother-in-law broke down in tears, overcome by the emotions of the moment. Soon, I was gazing out the airplane window, watching the sunrise from 35,000 feet in the air on New Year's Eve. Talk about new beginnings— this was one I hadn't expected.

When I walked into my father's house, the tension was palpable. At that time, he viewed being a committed Christian as a complete waste of time. In the past, he had often described my dedication to church as "crazy," "stupid," and an unnecessary distraction from making money and doing something "worthwhile." When I moved to the United States to attend Bible college, he'd told me I would fail and that one day he'd have to buy my plane ticket home. Now, he reminded me of those words, saying they had become self-fulfilling. He also mentioned he'd been drinking all weekend and blamed me for it.

He asked me to explain my struggles, and I began sharing my story openly. But within seconds, he became overwhelmed and walked away. No further conversation took place after that. In time, I believe he forgave me. What truly made a difference, though, was seeing that I had a good wife who loved me despite everything. Frankly.

She didn't care what others thought; her unconditional love held my family together and spared my parents and siblings from the pain of facing a potential divorce.

In the years that followed, my father's health deteriorated steadily. On the evening of March 11, 2020, around 8 PM, I made a spontaneous decision to buy a ticket to fly home for the funeral of a close friend, planning to return to New York on the 13th. Little did I know that day would become fateful—it was the last time I would see him alive. As I prepared to leave for the airport, he was in tears, and with a heavy heart, he told me it would be the last time. "I would see him again. "I believed him. As he lay in bed, I leaned in, hugged him, and kissed his forehead while tears streamed from his eyes. In a moment that will stay with me forever, I asked him to bless me, and he replied, "You are already blessed." Those words meant the world to me, especially given the turbulent relationship we'd had when I was younger. The change in his personality and behavior toward me was stark—night and day compared to the father I once knew, particularly after he learned of my struggles.

Looking back, I now understand that part of my father's frustration came from not having the words or emotional tools to talk to me about what I was going through. I can see his pain in retrospect, but at the time, I needed someone to talk to—someone who wouldn't judge me.

Unfortunately, the church I grew up in wasn't known for confidentiality. It was common for personal matters to become public knowledge. I'll never forget how, while outside of the U.S., I bumped into someone from the Midwest who knew my private business. It really is a small world, and not always in a good way.

Still, God placed it on my heart to reach out to a pastor friend in Trinidad. I told him I needed to talk, and without hesitation, he opened his home to me. I spent two weeks with him and his family, and it was one of the best decisions I made during that season of my life. Not everyone handles the reality of their life falling apart well. Many spiritual and mental forces sense the "blood" of your depression, circling like predators to consume your sanity, your dreams, and your sense of self-worth. As a relatively mature believer, I had the spiritual strength to fight back, but I needed to minister to myself. I remember sitting on a soccer field in Arima, Trinidad, listening to Yolanda Adams' songs on repeat, finding solace in every note. The words of the song are:

"keep the dream alive, don't let it die"

If something deep inside keeps inspiring you to try
Don't stop, and never give up; don't ever give up on You
Sometimes life can place a stumbling block on your way But
you've gotta keep the faith. Bring what's deep inside your
heart To the light And never give up; never give up on you
No, "don't give up."

That song meant so much to me. Knowing that my wife still loved and cared about me was a huge part of that "something deep inside keeps inspiring you to try; don't stop…." Many men suffer in silence, and some even suffer tragically, because the women who occupy the space in their hearts don't use their love as a beacon that inspires and transforms them into better versions of themselves. Every time she loves me right, something immortal comes alive within me. What do I mean by loving me right? Sex is at the bottom of the list. It's the words of life she speaks when I doubt myself, the way she cooks for me that brings a sense of comfort, her gentle touch, and her complete lack of any need to raise her voice at me. In almost 20 years of marriage, I can't recall a single instance where she's done that. Her capacity for forgiveness is remarkable—not just with me, but with others who've wronged her. Often, I see people coming back into her life, trying to make amends, likely because it's hard to stay bitter toward someone who treats you with kindness despite everything.

Watching all these traits manifest so early in our marriage gave me tremendous hope, especially knowing she felt betrayed that I hadn't shared everything with her up front, things she would have needed to know to decide if I was truly someone worth marrying. Yet, she stayed connected with me, constantly reaching out and giving me strength. Through this experience, my wife has shown me, whether intentionally or not, that the unconditional love of God is real. It has helped me understand why Christ sacrificed His life for humanity.

It was incredibly challenging being married and living in one country while my wife was in another. One day, I was texting her when I suddenly heard my mother pull into the driveway and honk her horn. I went to the balcony to see what she wanted, only to see my wife stepping out of the car. They had pulled one over on me! I was thrilled— the surprise was a total success. Soon after, everyone conveniently had "errands" to run, leaving us alone at home. I'll leave it to your imagination to guess what happened next (smile). Genesis 1:31: "…it was good…."

It wasn't easy for me. Even though I was surrounded by people, I felt self-conscious and lonely, and I had to be cautious about who I let close to me. I remember sitting in a powerful prayer meeting that challenged and unsettled me as my senses suddenly awakened to the boundless power of God. In that moment, I became deeply aware of His promises and faithfulness. The problem was that it didn't align with my real-world experience. Sitting on the pew, I challenged God. Frustrated, I told Him, "You and I need to talk." Driving home, my emotions only intensified. I went into my room, sat on the bed, and gave God an ultimatum.

At that time, it hadn't rained in weeks, and the land was bone dry. I sat there and said, "If I'm going through all this just to have my life crash and burn despite my faith and service to you, tell me now." I continued, "Who you are and what you can do is not matching up to the life I'm experiencing. If my life is truly going to be a success, as you've promised, make it rain in 10 minutes." I set a 10-minute countdown on my cell phone, folded my arms, and watched as the time ticked down. Five, four, three, two, one—and like clockwork, it began to rain, pouring cats and dogs. I sat there, my face frozen in amazement and wonder. As the rain came down with intensity and perfect timing, I called my wife and told her what had happened. God was assuring me that everything would be okay, as He'd promised, and that we needed to have faith and not worry.

I have held onto that moment as a pivotal life event, a sign pointing in the right direction. It has comforted me through the difficult times that lay ahead. Even though we were apart, God was doing a great work in each of us, strengthening us and connecting us by teaching us to communicate with one another more deeply.

Often, we communicate well with others but struggle to connect on a similar, deeper level with those we love. I couldn't find the words to tell my wife that, after God, she was the cornerstone restoring my life. We would talk, but the conversations didn't go deep enough. I would tell her sometimes that I just didn't have the words to express what I wanted to say. When I did try, it often came out wrong or got misinterpreted. Figuratively, it was like being told on a plane to put your own oxygen mask on first before helping your child. I became so focused on putting on my "oxygen mask"—thinking my wife was okay—that I missed the fact that she needed me more than ever. The shame I felt was incredibly deep and damaging, and I became preoccupied with salvaging and rebuilding myself. It's taken me years to give myself permission to feel happy again. Even though I knew God's word says we are healed, forgiven, and victorious, I struggled. Outwardly, I expressed belief. But inwardly, chains of regret, embarrassment, and failure kept me from thriving.

As a trained musician and singer, it took tremendous effort to allow myself back onto the platform to minister to others. My wife was my biggest champion through it all. I needed this because, deep down, I always wondered what others thought. In those early weeks after everything came to light, my wife told me that, in church, prayers were offered up to "rebuke the spirit of homosexuality from the congregation." It hurt. But I understand why they felt that prayer was necessary.

We're all on a journey of growth, and just as I am learning, so is my church family. We still attend the same church, and I still serve there. But occasionally, my thoughts wander to what others might think. Time and again, mutual friends would ask my wife to be a godparent to their child while ignoring me. Another time, the pastor instructed the congregation to pray for the person next to them. I let someone pray for me, but when it was my turn to pray for them, they walked away. I understand. We're often taught that people can "transfer spirits" and that these things require caution.

Still, I hold firm to the belief that "greater is He that is in me than he that is in the world." I believe in loving your neighbor as yourself. I believe that the work of God's creation—humankind, as defined by Christ—can tread upon snakes and scorpions and over all the power of the enemy, and nothing shall by any means harm us.

The fear of demonic transference between two genuine believers is a misplaced and misguided perspective. There's a reason why Christ said to lay hands on the sick and they shall recover; some of those sick among us suffer from demonic interference in their lives. Place your hands on them and pray, and they shall recover. The Bible doesn't teach, "Lay hands on them, and you shall also get sick." Life is a practical affair. If we claim to have the love of Christ in us, then those around us need to see it in a genuine way. This is why I'm so grateful to my wife for loving me the way she did. Of all people, I needed to feel loved by her—especially her. This central principle is a recurring theme in my journey. During my time away, she prioritized staying connected to me and traveled many times to be with me. There were countless instances in our marriage where she carried me. Her worth is beyond rubies.

So where am I now? Some of you might wonder, has he been delivered? Is he still occasionally engaging in homosexual behavior? The answer is that God is still transforming my mind daily and teaching me to make the right choices. I'll share three of the many principles that have helped me.

Firstly, over the years, the grace of God has taught me transformative lessons, compounding my desire to live a holy life. In those early years, I would pray fervently, only to find my life and desires unchanged. I was binding and loosing all sorts of things. My focus was on commanding and controlling the spiritual atmosphere outside of me, but what I should have been doing was mastering the spiritual environment within. I needed to understand that I wasn't at the mercy of the devil, demons, or any other evil influence. Too often, preachers make believers feel as though they're at the mercy of demons, but this is simply wrong. Jesus made it clear beyond a doubt when He "took the keys of death, hell, and the grave," and also said, "Behold, I give you power to tread on snakes and scorpions, and over all the power of the enemy, and nothing shall by any means hurt you" (Luke 10:19).

When I finally understood that I was in charge of my world, and not the devil—as many churches preach— the atmosphere of my life changed almost overnight. That's not to say all my lusts disappeared, but the power of my will and my self-awareness grew. I could consciously control my mind and cooperate with God in real-time. It was a game changer. The Spirit of God began rebuilding the mechanisms in my thinking that shaped my choices.

Consequently, the second of many powerful shifts came when God began to reshape my understanding of His intention for man to choose his own destiny. I had to shed the baggage of learned helplessness that I'd picked up growing up in church. I began to realize that God has spent the entirety of Scripture—from Genesis to Revelation—pursuing and perfecting, through testing, man's ability to choose and make correct decisions. Before this, I went through a phase where I felt I had to outsource my ability to make choices to the Spirit of God. In reality, the Spirit's role is to bear witness to God's Word, which I've hidden in my heart—like a GPS saying, "Turn right, not left." But His job is not to make me turn right or left, to choose good or bad; I had to learn to choose for myself.

God taught me that man's ability to choose is a spiritual muscle, intentionally given by Him. I learned that God won't interfere with our circumstances unless we invite Him to. As free as salvation is, it is never given until we consciously make a choice to accept Jesus as our Lord and Savior. While this might seem basic, in reality, it's not. For me, God needed to take me deeper and teach me that my personal power to choose was a muscle. With each act of obedience, I discovered that this muscle grew stronger and stronger. With this newfound strength came transformation from within my heart and mind.

Dr. Caroline Leaf, one of the world's foremost Christian researchers on neuroplasticity, has produced video images of new neurons forming in the brain in real- time while an individual actively learns. "As a man thinks, so is he" (Prov 23:7).

The third lesson that strengthened my mind is the simple principle of "whatever happens, don't stop; keep moving forward." Practically speaking, there are times when my mind drifts toward the wrong things. But my testimony is that God truly provides a way of escape. I cannot recall a time when my mind wandered without, in that same instant, the Spirit of God saying, "Snap out of it, just keep going." Without fail, I'd experience His Spirit redirecting my attention back where it needs to be, like flipping a switch each time. It's like an athlete sprinting down the track who suddenly falls—yet instead of quitting, they get up and keep running, only to win the race in the end. It took years for me to reach this place, and it hasn't been an easy journey. But God is real, and He is true. If I keep my trust in Him, there is no way I could fail.

Most people in the body of Christ tend to distance

themselves from brothers and sisters who have same-sex attraction. Their first response is often to throw 50 scriptures at you, as if that alone will somehow change everything. But it doesn't work that way. The truth is, many well-meaning believers lack the language and understanding to discuss this topic with someone on this journey. They often respond from a place of embarrassment, hurt, or indifference, sometimes struggling with their own personal battles.

Conversely, some believers blend political correctness with the Word of God and become overly tolerant. The reality is that, as believers today, if you have a child in my situation, love them unconditionally—but remember, God's ways and teachings are always right. Don't be ashamed to share that belief above all. Nothing we do surprises God. Absolutely nothing. His mercy is boundless, and each one of us is shaped by His hands. Whatever the enemy has crafted for evil, if we cooperate with God, even the most challenging and perplexing situations will work for our good and His glory. We can never outdo God in healing our moral struggles. He is that rope we reach for in the darkness; hold onto it for dear life, believing it will lead to the light, even if all you see in the moment is darkness. God cannot fail. This is my testimony.

A Letter to My Husband

After my husband finished writing, I read it, having intentionally arranged for us to work separately. I wanted his thoughts, feelings, and experiences to come through unfiltered, uninfluenced by anything I might have written. Even after 18 years of marriage, his words moved me deeply. Reading his chapter, I cried—he had expressed more about his inner world in those pages than he ever had before. As I absorbed his perspective, I felt our spirits intertwine even more, sharing in the pain he had carried for so long. I asked him, "Do you feel better now?" He gave me a sheepish smile and simply said, *"Yes."*

Through his writing, I gained a deeper insight into his soul, his thoughts, insecurities, fears, and doubts. His vivid memories, often of things I had forgotten, amaze me. Whenever he shares these details, he looks at me and shakes his head, wondering how I could forget something so significant. We always end up laughing about it. For instance, I didn't remember pulling my hand away from him during a car ride, but reading his words, I knew it was true.

He revealed things I had never known. My heart melted as I read, experiencing several "Oh my goodness" moments. I realized how much I truly meant to him, how my support had been a lifeline for him. I am so glad I stayed by his side. I often think about what life would have been like for both of us if I had left. Though he wasn't available when I finished reading, my first instinct was to hug him. Now, I see him through an even more loving and understanding lens, appreciating his ongoing fight to stay true to his values and beliefs. He chose God, and so did I. Hooray for us!

Since then, we've had many conversations about what we wrote. He shared how there were things in my chapter he hadn't known—my feelings and perceptions of the situations we lived through. He also admitted to making many mistakes early in our marriage. This was the communication I had longed for from the beginning. But now, even in the silence, I can see that God was at work all along, orchestrating everything with a purpose and a plan.

To my husband, I say this:

I am so incredibly proud of you and honored to be called your wife. God knew exactly what you needed when

He chose me for you, and He equipped me for this journey. I remember during our wedding ceremony; a prophetic word was given; the pastor said the one word he heard for us was *"Grace."* At the time, I didn't fully understand it, but now, looking back, I see how much grace God gave us to navigate this journey together. We couldn't have done it without Him. And if it's even possible, my capacity to love you has grown even more than it did back then.

I can hardly contain my excitement for what lies ahead. You have come through with flying colors, and now it's your time to make your mark—to share your story, bringing healing and hope to others. The enemy can no longer condemn you. I will always be right by your side, just as I know you'll be by mine. You'll never have to wonder where I am in the crowd. You will hear me cheering and see me waving your name on a flag. Everyone will know that I am your wife, proud and loud.

I am so grateful that you allowed me to share my side

of our story with the world, despite knowing the scrutiny and criticism it might bring, especially to you. But I am confident that God has our backs. We both understand our assignment, and while some may feel uncomfortable with our story, we know this is God's purpose for us, and nothing and no one can stand above that. As we fulfill His purpose, helping others, I trust God will also work on the hearts of those we care about—and even on our enemies.

I understand the wilderness period you endured because I had to go through mine as well. We were being pruned and prepared for today. We needed to learn life's lessons first, so we could be equipped to teach others and do it well. Who God sends; He qualifies. I already see doors opening for us and new connections being made along the way.

Your family loves you; my family loves you, especially my parents, and that will never change. I remember your father's words: *"You are already blessed."* Hold on to that. Don't let anyone define who you are. Your past is behind you, and it only holds power over your present if you allow it. Focus on where you're going by walking the path God has set for you—not the path of others who can't see how

God will use you or where He is taking you.

Challenges are part of life, but when you feel down, just imagine me singing and dancing for you. I promise it will make you laugh, especially when I do my Beyoncé moves! You have already proven your strength. When mountains seem impossible to climb or move, you find a way through. Keep building your inner strength, and never stop believing in yourself as much as I believe in you.

You are a man of integrity and dignity, with a big heart, bringing excellence to everything you do. I'm still in awe of how you managed to get straight A's while working full-time, attending college, and captivating all your professors. The sleepless nights you endured were all for us. You've always said, *"I'm not doing this for myself but for us,"* and I love you for that. God has truly gifted you— embrace it!

You've helped many people throughout your life, but that's nothing compared to the lives you'll impact through this book. Most of them we may never meet, but God created you in His likeness, and you walk in that truth. Some people come into our lives only for a season, but there's always something to learn. Have no regrets. God is your great reward.

I know I've listened to things said about you that, in hindsight, I shouldn't have entertained, and for that, I ask your forgiveness. We've both grown so much over the years, and we're still growing, becoming more like our Lord and Savior, Jesus Christ. I'm still learning how to love you fully, and I hope I continue to inspire you to be the best version of yourself. We've learned from each other and from our past. We will still make mistakes, but our goal is to make fewer and to never take each other for granted.

Great things lie ahead for us as a power couple. What the enemy thought was finished has only just begun. To God be the glory!

Life is full of unexpected challenges, but as James 1:2-8 (NIV) reminds us: *"Consider it pure joy, my brothers and sisters, whenever you face trials of many kinds, because you know that the testing of your faith produces perseverance. Let perseverance finish its work so that you may be mature and complete, not lacking anything. If any of you lacks wisdom, you should ask God, who gives generously to all without finding fault, and it will be given to you. But when you ask, you must believe and not doubt, because the one who doubts is like a wave of the sea, blown and tossed by the wind. That person should not expect to receive anything from the Lord. Such a person is double- minded and unstable in all they do."*

As we face the challenges ahead, we will stand firm on God's word, always asking for wisdom and never doubting His promises. We will soar on wings like eagles, run and not grow weary, walk and not faint (Isaiah 40:31, NIV).

We've got this, honey, and I love you beyond measure.

Your wife-Maxine

EPILOGUE

How did we overcome and where are we now?

It was important for us to acknowledge and accept the betrayal that happened, as uncomfortable and painful as it was. This was the first step toward healing for both of us. As mentioned before, I followed this with forgiveness to lighten my emotional burden. We confronted the issues in our marriage, and my husband began individual therapy, which, though it came later on, has helped him tremendously. As we gained understanding, we exercised patience with each other and learned to see things differently. I took time to grieve and process my feelings. Though difficult, having space between us allowed us to think retrospectively about our marriage and clarify what we truly wanted. Most of all, experiencing the love of God enabled me to love my husband when he needed it most, as we healed together. We are both better people today, and we eagerly look forward to the doors God will open and the exciting journey ahead as we help others through our story.

It brings me immense joy to say that my husband and I have come a long way. We have developed the art of communicating openly and without fear, making an extra effort to understand each other's needs and serve one another selflessly. We are genuinely happy and always look forward to spending quality time together. Traveling remains one of our favorite things to do, and we're blessed to have the opportunity to do so often. Our shared short- and long-term goals bring excitement into our relationship as we plan, execute, and watch these goals become realities. We find joy in encouraging each other to be our best and in supporting each other's dreams. We continue to serve God joyfully, seeking wisdom as we navigate life's uncontrollable challenges. Our emotional trust in each other is now unwavering, making it easy to share our feelings—good or bad. Each day is filled with continued growth and transformation. The safety and security I yearned for in the early years of our marriage, I can now say with certainty, I have found!

www.ingramcontent.com/pod-product-compliance
Lightning Source LLC
Chambersburg PA
CBHW070722010826
48977CB00006B/394